THE LEGEND

Totally forbidden territory for a girl engaged to be wed—that's Dr Bram Markland with the roving eye and lethal lifestyle. Just when her fiancé is injured and needing her, Staff Nurse Helen Westcott finds that Markland is planning to step in and do a smooth take-over . . .

THE LEGEND OF DR MARKLAND

BY

ANNA RAMSAY

MILLS & BOON LIMITED
15–16 BROOK'S MEWS
LONDON W1A 1DR

CHAPTER ONE

BLUE BEACONS revolving and headlights dipped, the ambulance wove an efficient passage through the line of motorists. The wail of the two-tone horns warned cars ahead to clear the road.

The ambulance driver was a young woman. She thrust a confident foot hard down on the accelerator, while inside the vehicle the emergency medical team braced themselves against the fresh surge of speed. Staff Nurse Westcott gripped the bench-seat with clenched fingers. Beneath the upswept corn-gold hair the tiniest crease of anxiety puckered her broad calm brow. The usual emergency team had been called out to a motorway smash; she and the doctor had been sent from the Accident and Emergency Unit in their place. A dramatic start to her first week at St Leonard's . . .

As the van swayed the piecrust edging of her new muslin cap trembled delicately, outward manifestation of the trepidation that speeded her heartrate and belied the serenity of her gentle, graceful features.

Helen had the face of a girl who never thinks an unkind thought. All the same, she was nobody's fool. And Bram Markland's undisguised perusal was little short of insolent . . . trapped as she was in a racing ambulance with a professional ladykiller—the darling of the hospital grapevine. Speeding towards her first-ever emergency 'blue call'.

The vehicle swayed on a sharp bend and Helen's long legs shot out of control. Her grey-and-white striped dress rode up over her elegant knees, affording the most undignified display of shapely round thighs in neat black stockings. The senior casualty officer wedged himself against the bulkhead, hoisted the merest trifle those lazy eyelids that had all the nurses swooning. Surveyed the provocative expanse of sheer black nylon with an expressionless stare that was not the slightest bit apologetic. And his hard mouth stayed clamped and sullen.

What a humourless character! Helen had expected to share a wry grin, but thought better of it. In its place she assumed what she hoped was a suitably haughty look, pressed her knees together, and presented Markland with an unabashed profile. If he was anticipating more of that impromptu cabaret, then he would be disappointed.

'Scared?'

The girl blinked as the drawled word registered, turned a puzzled face towards the doctor. 'I beg your pardon?'

He was grasping the safety handle, his left hand investigating the pockets of his white coat. Surely not a smoker? queried Helen silently. Disapproval illuminated her expressive face. Had not most doctors wisely kicked the habit? It was bad enough watching Dad puffing away towards an early grave.

But whatever it was, Bram hadn't found the object of his search.

His eyes settled once more on Helen's person, the heavy lids speculative and mocking. 'Your first week on A and E and Elsie Guppy chooses *you* to join me on a GOK mission. I take it you're more capable than you look.'

Helen gasped at this outrageous observation. Bram was staring rudely and most pointedly at her immaculate blonde head, the highly polished shoes, the meticulously hand-pressed uniform. For all the world as if being clean and tidy meant a nurse would not care to mess herself up coping with an industrial crush injury. 'Hardly a GOK mission, is it?' she asked coldly. 'Since we've had a radioed message warning us what to expect.'

This sensible but chilly reply seemed to goad the doctor on to further excesses of rudeness. '*So* sorry, Staff. Mustn't say God Only Knows in front of *you*, must we? Not in front of our revered chaplain's little daughter.'

So that was it! Bram Markland considered her a prissy little vicar's daughter, who would be bound to find his Lothario image distasteful . . .

Wait till he found out she was engaged to the Curate! An irrepressible smile lifted the corner of Helen's full mouth; as if she gave a fig for Bram Markland's legendary exploits. What did the others see in the fellow anyway? In comparison with darling Paul—who was not only her father's curate but also a visiting chaplain at St Leonard's—the casualty officer was singularly offputting. The two men were probably already acquainted, knowing Paul and his rugger scrum injuries: Bram Markland must have been obliged to patch him up a time or two.

Helen's secretly knowing smile intensified to a grin of disbelief as her eyes lighted upon Dr Markland's feet. Left foot black, right foot a nice shade of plum. And his plaid shirt looked as if it had spent the night on someone's bedroom floor. The medics didn't go about like *that* at the Royal Hanoverian. Life was clearly going to prove more casual in a Midlands teaching hospital.

She allowed her good-humoured blue gaze to drift upward, catching in Bram an answering flash of interest; just as if he had been expecting her to burst into tears—

and was intrigued by her more stolid reaction to his unkindness.

'If I tell you I was gold medallist of my PTS year at the Royal Hanoverian, I hope that may set your mind at rest.' Trying to maintain eye-contact with calm and dignity was none too easy when you were clinging to your seat and striving to keep your skirt at a decent level of coverage.

'Well, well. And doubtless there's a halo along with that awesome gold medal.' The doctor's mouth tightened into a grim line of satisfaction at the way that fair head tilted back—just as if he'd reached down and slapped her across the face. So neat and blonde and ladylike this new staff nurse . . . if his fingers tugged the pins out of that luxuriant hair, as they itched to, would it tumble right down to her waist? God Almighty but this was one devil of a hangover . . . where the devil had he put those pills? The two regarded each other with almost tangible dislike. So that's how you slay your ladies, thought Helen grimly. With that rapier-thrust repartee. Ever heard of charm, Dr Markland? What on earth do they all see in you?

It was a depressing prospect. From now on every working day was going to bring her into contact with this objectionable character. Thank heaven for the prospect of two days off duty, coming up at four p.m. She pulled out her fob watch, just an hour and a half to go. Oh it had better be worth it, swopping three of the happiest years of her life at the Royal Hanoverian, to come to St Leonard's where she could be near her fiancé once again. It wasn't that she wanted to twist Paul's arm about the wedding date; but he was a busy man, and if Helen was out of sight then she feared their wedding was not uppermost in his mind.

Helen gave her watch a little shake, as if wishing to speed up time. Her mind went back to the memory of her earliest visits to St Leonard's—for she was no stranger to this city which had been home since she was a toddler. Every Christmas Day Dad had carried her with him round the wards, and she had stood on a chair at the top table in the staff canteen while he had carved the first slice of the turkey and pronounced the Christmas blessing. And in the end there had been three little girls wide-eyed with wonder at the sights and bustle of the hospital; three little sisters all growing up determined to be nurses with white caps and aprons over their uniform dresses, just like the ladies they had marvelled at as children every Christmastide.

She was far away, lost in the dreams and aspirations of yesterday, her eyes dreamy and her gentle face relaxed—and a little sad . . .

'I asked you a question,' repeated the casualty officer, with brutal lack of concern for the new staff nurse's dignity. 'You did *not* have the courtesy to answer.'

When Helen was cross or under stress her eyes would deepen almost to purple, the pupils reducing to a mere pinprick. Bram noted the clinical signs of anger and dislike, and raised an interrogative brow. Women didn't often look at him like that, so undisguisedly, and survive to tell the tale.

He grinned wolfishly and his mahogany eyes glowed red. It gave Helen quite a fright, that reddish ember in the rich brown depths. Trapped and hostile, her gaze was locked with his. She would *not* look away.

'Scared of what, Doctor?' she snapped recklessly. 'The speed? The emergency?' *Or you* . . . Though by nature a placid, kind-hearted girl, this man had succeeded remarkably well in disrupting her equilibrium. But if the two of them were to establish some sort of working relationship, then she had all the confidence and pride of the qualified SRN. And no doctor was going to treat her as if she was no more than a professional hand-maiden. Bram Markland looked and sounded just the type to try.

Smoothly they negotiated a roundabout and accelerated briskly away. Markland bent his lanky height to view the road ahead through the cab window. He seemed in no hurry to answer her own question, though it hung between them with its clipped and rhetorical demand.

They were turning off the main roads now, striking into the heart of an industrial estate. In the quiet roads the driver extinguished beacon and horn, pulling up to a standstill behind another ambulance already parked outside a big paint factory. Tension flared up, in spite of her determination to remain calm, as Helen grabbed her share of the essential apparatus and followed Bram through the rear doors. Presumably he would prove more admirable as a surgeon than as a person. Well, she should quickly find that out; just as in his eyes her own competence and nerve were going to be tested.

An agitated reception party of blue-overalled men was waiting impatiently at the factory gates. They surrounded the nurse and doctor, their thankfulness touching Helen's soft heart.

'What happened?' Bram was brusque and in control, his eyes flicking to the police car racing up behind them.

'It's Dave from the filling shop,' stuttered their spokesman. 'D-Dave Hemby. This 800-litre paint vat just sort of slipped off the hoist.' Helen winced and Bram gave a low whistle. She felt sick, her throat tight and dry as the desert.

'Let's get on down there.' Bram loped along on his

lanky legs and Helen followed close behind. It was bitterly cold and she hadn't stopped to fetch her cloak. She regretted that now, shivering as she pictured the crush injuries that awaited them.

Bram hung back and muttered for her ears only. 'If we're picking up a DOA, I'm going to create merry hell. Do they think I've nothing better to do?'

Helen reacted to this with silent anger. Heartless beast! Of course you'd rather be back on Casualty lording it over the living, surrounded by gooey-eyed handmaidens. She trotted along at his heels, her arms full of packages and her heart full of dread.

Markland was tall and very thin. You could see the shape of his shoulderblades through the fabric of his white coat. He was rather stooped, like many a tall surgeon. She wondered if he could feel the dagger of her eyes, for she was aiming for the very centre of his self-important back . . .

An ambulanceman came forward to greet them. *He* didn't seem too much in awe of the casualty officer anyway, Helen noted thankfully. Though he was clearly glad enough to see him. Doubtless Bram only got pleasure out of scourging defenceless nurses!

'What have you got for me this time, Arthur?'

'Oh and what about me? Am I the invisible woman all of a sudden?' muttered Helen to no one in particular, bristling at Bram's exclusive enquiry.

'Crush injuries, Dr Markland. Pulse and respiration high. Open fracture of left tibia. We've put the leg in an air splint and started the Entonox.'

'That's the ticket.' Bram loped over to his patient leaving Helen to hump the emergency equipment. At his approach the huddle of men in their paint bespattered overalls fell back in silent awe. For goodness' sake—he's just a fellow who specialises in human mechanics, Helen longed to scold—you don't have to tug your forelocks and look so humble.

She sank to her knees on the bone-shattering concrete, wincing as the cold hardness drove into her patellae. Then all thoughts of discomfort vanished as she studied Dave Hemby with astute professional concern. All the classic symptoms of surgical shock: the pallor of the cold clammy skin, the breath coming in rapid shallow pants of air hunger. Every smallest observation must be recorded for the hospital files.

Meanwhile Bram was pumping morphine sulphate into Dave's bloodstream with one swift injection. The relief was almost immediately apparent. The man had been clutching desperately to the Entonox mask, through which he was inhaling an analgesic mix of oxygen and nitrous oxide. Now as the waves of pain diminished he could relax his grasp and let the mask fall away from his face. 'Water!' he gasped weakly, 'please . . . water.' His searching tongue dragged pitifully over dry cracked lips.

Helen leaned over so Dave could see her face as she spoke to him. Her eyes made reassuring contact with his. 'I can't give you anything to drink, Mr Hemby, you may need an anaesthetic soon. But you have nothing to worry about—Dr Markland from St Leonard's Hospital is here to take care of you.'

Pallid and sweating, the injured man managed a weary nod of acquiescence. It occurred to Helen he must be about the same age as her father, plumper though and less grey; clean-shaven where her father was bearded.

'Squeeze Nurse's hand if I'm hurting you, Dave,' ordered the doctor in brisk unemotional tones. His exploratory fingers probed deep into flesh and muscle, palpating the abdomen where the overalls had been drawn aside. Dave shrank and groaned and his finger-nails sunk into Helen. She glanced sharply at Bram and he whispered to her to make brief notes as he dictated.

Helen reached for pad and pencil and indicated she was ready.

'Rib fracture here on the left—directly over the spleen. I can feel the swelling underneath . . . no, don't write *that*, you prune!'

Helen cursed beneath her breath and glowered as she scrubbed out the last half-dozen words. How was she expected to know when he was just thinking aloud?

'The spleen's ruptured and there is internal haemor-rhage . . .' She scribbled as fast as she could manage with fingers getting bluer by the minute, until Bram was satisfied with his on-the-spot diagnosis. 'Get a blood sample sent on ahead for cross-matching. And have the Emergency Room alerted. We must introduce fluids now before his veins collapse completely from shock and internal haemorrhage.' He started the struggle to insert a cannula into non-existent veins in the back of the patient's hand, while Helen took a litre bag of normal saline and, as speedily as was humanly possible, began to run the fluid through the connector.

'Damn it. This is hopeless!' Bram abandoned his attack on Dave's hand and turned his attention to the inside of the elbow. He applied a tourniquet, briskly stroked the flaccid arm, peered with frustration at the injection site. 'I can't see a vein,' he complained. 'Have to go for pot luck . . .'

Both doctor and nurse breathed sighs of relief as the tiny cannula slid into position in an undiscernible vein.

The saline was ready—apart from a few remaining air

bubbles. Helen flicked at them with deft experienced fingers.

'For God's sake, woman! You're not at the Royal Hanoverian now. Pass me that.'

Across Dave Hemby's defenceless head two pairs of eyes met in challenge; hers deepening to purple-blue as her indignation simmered steadily. His glinting darkly with impatience.

'This man needs fluids—and fast.'

'Do you think I don't know it, Dr Markland? We were taught always to get rid of *all* air bubbles.' Helen's soft mouth compressed into a steely line of determination. She was not going to be goaded into losing her temper, and certainly not across the prone person of a patient haemorrhaging internally and with a dire need to get fluids into his collapsed veins and arteries. If Markland was seeking to get her riled, then he was about to be disappointed. For the moment.

The doctor's head was bent, limp brown hair—he could do with visiting a decent barber—flopping over his forehead as he drew a syringeful of blood before connecting up the IV line. He spoke as he worked, looking not at Helen but at what his hands were doing. His tone was didactic but conversational. 'A few air bubbles really won't hurt, you know. The human body can take up to a syringeful of air before it starts causing problems.'

The staff nurse had a most attractively determined chin. And an unconscious habit of thrusting out her lower lip as she tilted her head up. A lesser girl would have been so vulgar as to sniff: *that* sort of sloppy procedure was not the way things were done at the Royal Hanoverian . . . still, if Dr Markland *was* right—and he ought to know, she grudgingly conceded—it was only proper to appreciate his concern to share with her information that could one day come in useful. In an emergency, it was clearly vital to know where one might safely cut the odd corner.

Helen handed over to George's keeping the saline bag and hauled herself up off achingly frozen knees. She collected the blood sample and her scribbled notes and took both over to the waiting policeman. 'If you could get these to St Leonard's as fast as possible,' she requested. 'This chap's going to need urgent surgery.'

They took Dave Hemby out to the waiting ambulance, strapping him securely to a fracture board and lifting him gently in a scoop stretcher. Helen walked at his side holding high the saline infusion. Dr Markland had disappeared, but Helen assumed that as it was an industrial accident there must be forms he had to sign for the insurance. They got Dave safely aboard, fastened him to the red-blanketed trolleybed, and Helen was just looking anxiously round to spot the doctor when he appeared out of nowhere, raising a laconic eyebrow as he noticed her pale face pressed to the dark glass of the window.

He slumped into a corner, well out of her way. The two ambulance staff were riding in the front of the van. But Markland had positioned himself so the nurse's every move was under effortless observation. It seemed best to pretend he wasn't there, rather than let that constant scrutiny make her self-conscious. So Helen ignored him and concentrated her undivided attention on Mr Hemby.

The fractured tibia, nasty wound though it was, was no immediate problem, covered by sterile dressings and cushioned in an air splint. The drip had been fastened to the side of the stretcher, leaving the nurse with her hands free to keep a check on pulse and blood pressure, and regulate the saline infusion.

Still those lazy-lidded eyes scrutinised her person and every smallest task she performed. Helen was grateful the procedures were so routine she could have carried them out blindfold. It was foolish to let oneself be bothered by the doctor's rude habit of staring. If only the channel of her spine would stop that ridiculous tingling . . .

An enormous yawn shocked her into turning round and acknowledging that he was there. Markland's head was lolling, his eyes blank with fatigue. Well, he would get no sympathy from anyone the way he was reputed to carry on . . .

Her voice was severe. 'You look as if an early night would do you no harm, Dr Markland.'

Bram opened his eyes and responded with a sour curl of the upper lip. He was either tired or bored—or both.

'A good night's *sleep*, Doctor. Or perhaps you don't get sufficient fresh air and exercise.' His skin, decided Helen, doing a bit of close observation herself, was that kind of sallow which is much improved by a brisk walk over the moors—or a boisterous game of rugby football. Her imagination pictured Paul—so tall, so handsome with his strong regular features, his clear healthy skin and that thick soft head of golden curls. His muscle-packed athlete's frame and the whites of his grey eyes brilliant with health.

She settled her fingers over Mr Hemby's pulse, checking the second hand on her fob watch, entered her findings on the chart she had begun for the records.

'Perhaps you are a squash man, Dr Markland,' she suggested to break the heavy silence.

Bram recoiled visibly. 'Squash? *Squash!*' He made it sound like a bad case of herpes.

'Well,' Helen battled on valiantly, 'most people like to take some form of exercise these days . . .'

He wasn't really listening, just enjoying himself examining her figure in a manner that was less compliment and more affront. Helen wondered what he found wrong with it, she hadn't had many complaints so far. Too thin probably for his taste. Still, keep trying to be amiable— no one is all bad, so they say. 'Personally I enjoy aerobics, or a foursome at badminton.'

'A twosome's more to my taste,' leered Bram, brightening visibly at the sound of his own wit. His grin was sudden and the reluctant beholder found herself fascinated and revulsed at one and the same time. Those surprisingly nice teeth, irregular with slightly pointed incisors, strong and white looking. The engaging lopangled twist of that derisive mouth . . . shame it belonged to such an unpleasant character.

'There's just one form of exercise *I* go in for, Staff. And if you haven't already heard what that is, then the grapevine at St Leonard's must be in dire need of a drip feed of juicy gossip. Any skeletons in your cupboard eh, Staff? Or are you going to leave all the fuelling to us poor doctors?' That hypnotic voice of his was rich was sarcasm as the hard eyes summed up Helen Westcott with her immaculate uniform and the calm clear conscience backing up that air of serenity.

Why can't you leave me alone? Helen turned a rebellious back on the hopeless case Dr Markland presented. She absorbed her attention in checking and recording blood pressure levels . . . then gave a gasp and a start of surprise to find Bram Markland's hand resting firmly and without apology on her waist. In the confined space by their patient he was standing so close behind her she could feel the heat from his body warm against her back. In words that typically suggested she was the one getting in the way, he told Helen to give him a bit of space . . . whereupon she leapt away and squashed herself up against the window, her bare elbow against the icy glass. The imprint of his hand was still there on her flesh, as though it had burned through her clothes to the skin beneath. She pressed her own hand wonderingly to the spot—then, chiding herself for a fool, let it drop before she was observed by those X-ray eyes.

A small frown creased Bram's forehead as he bent over Dave. Could he have missed something from that earlier diagnosis? It would be unusual to have made even a minor error. Was something new developing, a fresh threat to Dave's already grave condition?

Helen saw the look on his face and, any self-consciousness all forgotten, touched the doctor's sleeve in silent enquiry.

Bram straightened, and massaged his bony jawline with a thoughtful hand. Without X-rays he could not be a hundred per cent sure. He turned to the nurse with a helpless lift of the shoulders. 'Don't much care for the breathing sounds on the left side of the chest. Could be a pneumothorax there.' Once more he positioned the bell of his stethoscope on the man's chest and listened intently.

Helen peered through the window and out into the lights of the city. Not far to go now.

At that moment Mr Hemby groaned and doctor and nurse drew close to his side. He opened his eyes and stared in bewilderment at the cream roof of the ambulance. Whatever calamity had befallen him? The pretty face of a blonde nurse was smiling down into his, her comforting hand enclosing his cold one. Strange how cold his limbs were . . . and inside, somewhere near his ribs, there was a terrible and frightening sense of pressure . . . again that pain that made him groan aloud in agony. Dave opened his mouth and tried to speak to those two floating faces. The calm one moved nearer . . . face of an angel in heaven. Closer still, until the mouth was right there next to his ear. 'Don't try to say anything,' it was telling him, 'we're here to take care of you.'

He liked that other face too, it looked strong and confident and in charge. It wouldn't let anything bad happen. Now the mouth was opening and shutting . . . Dave listened and was comforted by the certainty of those words. All was going to be well, he would pull through this.

'Just hang on, Dave—in a couple of minutes you'll be in the hospital and Dr Markland will have you sorted out.' The nurse was wielding a syringe again . . . and seconds later Dave was drifting back into merciful oblivion.

'You'll be ready for this!' Sister Guppy set a mug of steaming coffee at Bram's elbow as he sprawled over a chair in her cramped little office. 'Want a snort in it?' With a knowing little smile she unlocked a cupboard and produced a bottle of brandy. 'For medicinal purposes only,' she added warningly, holding the bottle poised over his coffee.

A lean brown hand insinuated itself over hers and wickedly tipped the bottle to a steeper angle. 'Don't be stingy, Guppy. I'll still be in theatre long after you're tucked up for the night.'

Sister clucked over the dark circles under his eyes. 'Keep you out of mischief then, young man.' She stoppered the brandy firmly and locked it away again. 'I shouldn't care to hazard a guess as to what you were up to last night.'

A flicker of that lop-sided reminiscent grin which had turned many a nurse's bones to water . . . 'Since you're not a married lady, dear Guppy, that is an area we shall explore no further.

Elsie Guppy sniffed good-humouredly. 'Don't start getting considerate at this late stage in our relationship. Only *I* know you're not as lethal as you're made out to be. You wouldn't be much use here on Casualty as senior doctor if your reputation was a hundred per cent lived up to . . . and I'm thankful to say your private life has never yet been known to affect the high standard of your work. When it does, my dear Bram, be sure I shall let you know.'

Bram slurped his adulterated brew, keeping an admiring eye on the powerful yet diminutive figure in navy blue, setting her cap straight in front of the small mirror on the wall behind the filing cabinets and then moving to her big desk with its neat ranks of files and papers. A formidable lady, Elsie Guppy, who ran a difficult department as if born for the job.

'How's your work for the Fellowship exams coming along?'

Bram waved a dismissive hand as if he didn't wish to be reminded of the arduous extra studies involved in joining the College of Surgeons. 'Fine,' he said vaguely, 'fine.' He was waiting for his patient to be prepared for theatre—might as well relax, grab a few moments' shut-eye . . . He hoped the new staff nurse wouldn't hurry in her nervousness and make a mess of shaving Mr Hemby.

The small, secret smile went un-noticed by Sister, who was working through a pile of forms awaiting her attention. She was quite happy for Bram to doze in her office till he was called to theatre.

The smile lingered . . . However calm that young woman might seem on the surface, there were hidden depths Bram knew he'd been successful in igniting. He'd seen it in the way those blue eyes deepened almost to purple—the colour you got, he mused, recalling his Art lessons back at school, when you spilled just one drop of scarlet into blue. Oh yes, he'd got her mad all right, underneath that serene surface . . . that was fire right there in her eyes. Blue eyes and hair the colour of wheat, complexion the hue of a creamy Christmas rose. Bram suddenly knew what it was Helen had reminded him of all along. The gentle sweetness of a madonna, come down from an ancient stone niche in some mediaeval cathedral. Funny to think of a madonna doing a preop. shave . . .

He opened one eye and looked at Elsie Guppy.

'What's amusing you?' she demanded. 'Is my cap crooked or something?'

'Just thinking about our new staff nurse—'

Sister settled her wiry frame back into her chair and tapped a thoughtful pen against her teeth. 'How do you find her then, our new little staff nurse?'

'Not so little—next to you the girl's a strapping Amazon. Got legs up to here.' Bram waved an uncoordinated arm and knocked his empty coffee mug flying. 'Whoops!'

Sister sighed and got up to rescue her property, rinsing the crocks in her corner wash basin. A woman in her late forties she was tough and good-humoured, her brown hair neatly permed and greying. 'I've known Helen

Westcott since she was a youngster. If it hadn't been for me, she'd have ended up at university reading something useless like sociology or history.'

'A fate worse than death,' agreed Bram, running a hand through his untidy brown hair. He was overdue for a haircut—perhaps that redhead on Raphael Ward would give it another snip-over with her surgical scissors. One thing you could say about his cast-offs: they parted affectionately and went on adoring from afar. Well, those who didn't transfer their affections to that macho young hospital chaplain, Father Paul from Holy Trinity parish church. Next time that guy turned up in Casualty on a Saturday afternoon, expecting tea and sympathy for his rugger wounds, Bram was planning on stitching him up with water in the syringe instead of lignocaine!

As for the fair Helen . . . 'She's no dumb blonde, I'll give her that. Sharp edge to her tongue,' he added with relish. Then, grudgingly, 'Knows what she's doing— though she's over pernickety for my liking.'

'Remember she's trained at the Royal Hanoverian and their standards are exacting.' Sister frowned over the reference to her protégée's sharp tongue—it wasn't the most obvious thing about Helen, though she was certainly a witty and articulate girl. 'I hope you haven't been naughty, Bram. I promised Father Westcott that Helen would settle in happily in my Unit.'

Bram looked sour, pulling his lanky height from the depths of the only comfy chair. 'You and your crush on the Vicar,' he scoffed. Elsie however regarded him with bland composure. 'Phone the orthopods for me. George Raven said he was going to scrub too, and sort out that leg of Hemby's.'

'I think you'll find he's already here,' said Sister, 'since

I spoke to him twenty minutes ago. Now please be charming to Helen—all three of LBW's daughters are thoroughly nice girls.'

'*Nice* girls—ugh! Heaven preserve me from nice girls. Who christened the Vicar "LBW", anyway? Not you I daresay, Guppy. You'd never be so disrespectful of the cloth!'

Sister laughed and shook her head. 'That's Paul for you! Dear Father Paul, the curate. Great sportsman as you know—and the Vicar was quite a cricketer in his day. His initials you see, LBW. Actually, Paul is engaged to Helen Westcott—they'll make such a wonderful partnership. Can't you just picture their beautiful children?'

Seeing that Bram's jaw had dropped more than a little at this revelation, Sister added that this was the reason for Helen leaving London and taking her staffing post at St Leonard's: to be nearer her fiancé. 'I thought you knew that, Bram dear.'

He glowered over her diminutive figure as the two of them paused at the office door. 'Like hell I did. You mean to tell me that great mop-headed hunk who strolls round St Leonard's in a long black dress and steals my thunder is going to marry that ravishing—er hum!—sanctimonious Grace Kelly look-alike? Well . . . good luck to the both of them, say I.'

Sister concealed the twitch of her lips, saying with her hand reaching to open the door, 'How nice of you to wish them well, dear boy.'

'I'm off.' Bram ground his teeth with savage disgust and stamped away to the gowning and scrub-up area. So the maiden was not fair game after all, dammit.

Had the unpredictable surgeon been gifted with supernatural hearing, he might have enjoyed listening in to a conversation taking place on the other side of the wall as he vented his ire in a ferocious scrubbing ritual. For in the sluice, Helen and the senior staff nurse, Maggie Owen, were comparing notes. Casualty was slowing down, a lull settling over the department. Nobody was hurrying—and Sister was buried in her admin work, and likely to stay so occupied for the next half hour. Both girls had their hands wrapped about comforting mugs of hot sugarless tea.

'Well, that's your first and worst week over, Helen. Starting a senior job in an A and E department is living hell. I've been here three years now, but it's still etched on my memory, that awful first week. You don't know where things are kept, and you feel so inadequate when there's a hectic life-and-death rush on. Still,' she beamed at Helen over the rim of her mug, 'you've been amazing—our Elsie's ever so pleased. We were only saying this morning how you're one of the team, straight off and no fussing.'

Relief and happiness surged through Helen's weary frame. How good of Maggie to take the trouble to reassure a new and stumbling colleague. And what a delight and comfort she was to work with, this strongly built, plain-speaking woman of around the mid-twenties. Just the sort who wouldn't turn a hair when on a Saturday night the drunks and yobboes came rampaging into Casualty, tanked up to the eyeballs and nursing broken noses and split heads. Though her face was never her fortune, Maggie was blessed with a swinging healthy bob of glorious apricot hair, as romantic as the heart within that made no secret of her yearnings after Dr Bram Markland.

'Aren't you the lucky one—getting Bram all to yourself this afternoon. He's brilliant in Casualty—quick thinking, resourceful, never at a loss. And *such* a honey!'

Helen spluttered as her tea took a wrong turning. If Dr Markland was honey then heaven help the bees. He'd pinched all their stings and hurled them in her direction. No wonder she felt punctured and deflated after their encounter.

'I didn't find him all that friendly,' she said carefully. She hesitated a moment and then admitted the truth, 'Actually he doesn't much like me.'

'Rubbish!' said Maggie with clear disbelief.' Just look at you—course he likes you, Bram always make a beeline for the pretty ones. He's dated all the best-looking nurses. The man's a legend here at St Leonard's. They do say,' she added confidentially, 'that he'll never shoulder the responsibilities of marriage. Being free of ties means he can do as he pleases, give in to his roving eye. Wish his eye would roam my way for once!' She sat there on the worktop, drumming disconsolate heels on the cupboard fronts as she mulled over her longings. 'Still,' she grinned, 'we do have a laugh together over this and that.'

Helen looked faintly incredulous, but made a polite sound that could be interpreted as Maggie chose.

'And you've captured the glamorous Father Paul, so there's half Bram's competition gone. That ought to please him.'

'Maggie, what on earth do you mean?'

'Oh,' sighed the senior staff nurse, lighting up a sneaky cigarette and offering the packet to Helen who shook her head. 'Half the nurses are in love with Bram—the other half think your Paul is God's gift to the female sex. Oh sorry, Helen. I'm a bit of a plain speaker, being a Yorkshire lass and all that.'

The new staff nurse's face was a study. Of course her father and Paul, both of them being chaplains to St Leonard's, must be familiar faces in the wards and corridors. But to discover so many hearts yearning over one's fiancé was disconcerting to say the least. Well, more like *devastating*!

Not that Helen didn't trust Paul implicitly. He was so full of natural goodness and totally without vanity. As nice inside as he was to look at.

Dear Paul, everyone thought the world of him. Her parents, her sisters, the parishioners, the patients he came to visit. And so apparently did the nursing staff— though their interest was a little more predatory. Helen bit her lip and wondered if this was what jealousy felt like . . .

She said goodbye to Maggie and, 'See you in two days' time!' for she had the weekend off. Then went along to the locker room to change, pondering on Dr Markland and the events of the afternoon. He definitely did *not* approve of her, in spite of Maggie's kindly-meant re-assurances. And it seemed to be because of who she was, rather than what she was, judging by the snide and nasty barbs let fly in her direction.

Helen couldn't help feeling sad about this. It niggled and hurt to be so unkindly prejudged and sentenced. Still, perhaps it was as well to witness for one's self, right from the start, the darker side of the legendary ladykiller of St Leonard's. It should keep her on her toes if there were skirmishes to come . . .

CHAPTER TWO

ST LEONARD'S Hospital grew up around the workhouse buildings in what was once the poorest part of the city. It stands exposed to the elements on a high and windy hill, a sprawl of Victorian redbrick, with an apparently haphazard collection of modern buildings—including the block housing the Accident and Emergency Department—tacked on to the original pile. A rampart of modest terrace housing has replaced the old slums and is popular with hospital staff—particularly the nurses—in providing convenient flatlets for those who have outgrown the delights of the Nurses' Home and Home Sister's vigilant concern for the girls of the PTS.

Helen was one of those travelling farther afield. She wheeled her cycle out of the hospital gates, following other figures shrouded in warm red-lined capes with only a hundred yards or so to go before they reached home comforts. Helen had changed out of uniform for the ride home. To guard her ears against the spiteful January blast—for she had a tendency to get earache—she tied one of her mother's home-woven scarves snug about her head and turned up the collar on her navy jacket, buttoning it up tight to the throat. Crêpe-soled ankle boots and blue jeans completed an ensemble designed for comfort rather than elegance on the mile-and-a-bit downhill ride back to the parish of Holy Trinity.

It was lighting up time. Helen stooped over the handlebars to fiddle with her flickering front lamp.

Was it going to fail? One sharp rattle and the beam obligingly steadied.

Good old battle-stained warrior! How many years is it since you whizzed me back and forth to the High School, from trembling-kneed little first-year off to 'big school' for the first time—to sixth form prefect, proud as punch because I'd been accepted at the hospital of my dreams. 'Whoa, steady on there—remember I'm a wee bit out of practice! Though they say you never forget how to ride a bike . . .'

It was a matter of minutes before in the distance Helen spotted the sooty spire of her father's church, and in no time at all she was coming round the corner and there it was, the old redbrick vicarage, forbiddingly gaunt until you got inside among the homely clutter, with all those thousands of books spilling over into every room including the lavatory. The house fronted right onto the pavement, its garden—generous in a city—spreading alongside and round the back. Scene of many a fête and the games of generations of vicarage children, its grassy lawns were bleached and stiff with the winter's frosts, an old swing, forlornly rusting and abandoned now the girls were growing up.

Helen hopped off her bike outside the butcher's shop and waited for a gap in the traffic. A friendly hand waved to her from across the road as yet another parishioner beamed to see the vicar's eldest daughter back again from her London hospital. Such a pretty girl, so pleasant and kind—and engaged to that dear Father Paul. What a beautiful couple, what a perfect match!

Waving energetically back, Helen felt a surge of renewed pleasure overtake the inevitable fatigue which closes a nurse's working day. 'Hello there, Mrs Lock-wood. Nice to see you again!' It was so heartwarming to be back among familiar faces and familiar sights. Home sweet home—even though nothing could be farther removed from a picture postcard cottage with roses round the door. Mum had probably forgotten to shop for supper too; it wouldn't be the first time she'd got herself so absorbed in weaving or dyeing or painting that the oven was cold and the cupboard bare. Never mind, there was always fish and chips from Andy's down the road.

Even the smell of cigarette smoke wafting round the study door was welcoming. Dad always smoked when he was working at the typewriter. Nag as they all might, there was no curbing that habit of his, the vicar's only relief from the stresses of his calling.

Quietly Helen peeked round the door, not wanting to disturb if he was deep in thought. The usual organised chaos (at least that was what the vicar called it) met her eyes. Papers everywhere, the layout of the parish magazine spreading over a long trestle table, well-thumbed theological tomes ranged along every available bit of wall space. Nothing must ever be moved or tidied. Then and only then would her placid peace-loving parent blow his top. It meant the room was impossible to clean properly, but that was bottom on the Vicar's list of priorities. He claimed to be able to lay a hand on anything at a moment's notice.

Sensing another's presence, he looked up from pounding away at an ancient Olivetti, eyes crinkled against the smoke from one of a chain of Woodbines. 'Darling! You're back at last. How did it go today?'

In retrospect the day had not been so bad, if you put Bram Markland right out of mind. 'I'm settling in surprisingly quickly. Having a good memory helps, because you've got to know where all the equipment is kept so you can lay your hand on things at a moment's notice. Any spare second I have I put to good use, checking the cupboards and so on. Is Jenni back?'

'She's upstairs with your mother in the studio. Shall I make a cup of tea? Would you like one, dear? You must be worn out.'

'No no, just let me get my second wind and *I'll* make us all some.' Helen moved a pile of yellowing *Church Times* out of an easy chair and sat herself down for a moment. She pulled off her scarf and her hair fell down from its pleat in a heavy corn-coloured mass. 'I see you've been tidying up again!'

The Vicar caught his daughter's naughty teasing eye. 'Ha! ha!' he replied with dry humour. 'That'll be the day.' He stubbed his cigarette into an ashtray.

'Elsie Guppy was at the six o'clock service this morning. I told her I hope she's looking after my Staff Nurse.'

'His' staff nurse was unbuttoning her heavy jacket, kicking off her boots and stretching neat toes towards the meagre heat of the small gas fire. The place had no central heating. Even if they could have afforded the bills for such unsought-after comforts. Her father's fingers were blue and mottled with cold as he sat at his ancient typewriter; the sleeves of his cassock, on a wooden coathanger behind the study door, fraying and bound at the edges with her mother's neat stitches and a length of black petersham binding.

'Sister Guppy's being a poppet—and the rest of the team couldn't be kinder.' Helen hesitated over the little white lie, then couldn't resist adding with nonchalant pride, 'I went out to an accident this afternoon with the casualty officer, Bram Markland.'

Her father looked surprised. 'I thought you had a

special Emergency Medical team to deal with acci-
dents?'

'We have—but they were called out earlier to a motorway smash.' Her father shuddered for the hapless
victims and murmured 'Poor souls!'

'Have you come across Bram Markland, Dad?' Helen
asked casually.

'Bram Markland? I know the name, of course. But I
don't include Casualty on my visits. That's more Paul's
territory, seeing how he likes to spend Saturday afternoons there being patched up or deconcussed.'

'Oh Dad!' Helen forgot all about that 'of course'
attached to Bram Markland and latched on to her
fiancé's propensity for self-inflicted injury. For what else
could you call it when a grown man chose of his own free
will to volunteer in summer to face demon bowlers,
while in winter he loved nothing better than to risk his
precious neck in a rugger scrum. Helen had dealt with
her share of sports injuries too, and had come to recognise the medical world's increasing concern at the
dangerous elements in such 'games'.

'You would have thought being an Oxford Blue and
having the satisfaction of playing for your university
might have been enough for Paul. If you ask me, it's high
time he hung up his boots and retired with dignity. He's
lucky never to have been seriously hurt.'

'Don't grumble at him about it, darling,' the Vicar
advised mildly. 'Our Lord wants us to make use of *all* our
talents, and Paul is a gifted sportsman.'

'Our Lord doesn't have to wash his mud-caked gear,'
retorted she irreverently. Then with a twinkle in her eye,
'I say Dad—couldn't you bring Evensong forward on
Saturday afternoons, say from seven to three-thirty?
And tell Paul the Bishop has especially suggested he

must take the service as valuable experience?'

The Reverend Westcott grinned and rolled a fresh sheet of paper into his Olivetti. Whatever would Helen think of next! 'You dreadful child,' he chided. 'Our Paul is a natural athlete—it's in his blood. And a young priest needs to be able to let off steam sometimes. If you can't live with that,' the deeply lined face beneath its grizzled beard and thinning hair grew suddenly solemn as he regarded his daughter, perched there by the fire, her gentle face upturned, 'if you cannot live with that,' he repeated gravely, 'then don't, for heaven's sake, marry the poor man. I should dread to think of either of you making the other unhappy.'

Eyes, more cloud-grey than blue now, flashed her hurt and indignation. 'But Dad—I *am* proud of Paul. Really I am, how can you believe otherwise? You know me better than that. It . . . it's just that I'm afraid he may get badly injured one of these days.'

'You can't wrap the man up in cotton wool, my dear. And we have to give each other space to grow and develop as human beings. Do you understand what I mean by that?'

'I think so,' said Helen chastened and thoughtful. 'I'll go and make that tea now.'

Still pondering over her father's wise words, Helen wandered off to the kitchen . . . Heaven be praised! Two fresh-baked loaves of scofa bread and, coming from the oven, the pungent aroma of a simmering herby casserole. 'Mother!' declared Helen aloud, 'when you're in the mood your cooking is simply unsurpassable. Mmmm. Now—let's get that pot of tea brewing.'

Before the kettle could be filled a path must be fought to the kitchen taps. Ridiculous to have a room this small for a kitchen . . .

But the sink was occupied by a large stainless steel bucket, a special sort of bucket used only for mixing up dyes; brimming now with some weed-logged purplish concoction. It was a bit of a struggle, getting it out of the sink without any spillages . . . but Helen managed things successfully, long-accustomed to the household hazard of Mum and her buckets of dye. They tended to lurk in dark corners, the buckets, waiting to trip up the un-suspecting passer-by, threatening wiʌn their murky contents and ankle-scraping metallic edges.

Five minutes later, having set a mug with two sugars close by her father's typewriter, Helen was making her steady way, juggling three no-sugars up the creaking back stairs and along the passage to a large disused bedroom that her mother had converted into a studio. This room faced south and the light through the lofty vicarage windows was good for sewing and weaving and painting, and all the other creative activities at which Margot Westcott was so talented. Two huge wooden looms dominated the far corner, and over one of these bent two people who—observed from a distance—might have been sisters: smallish and fragile, the one an older and prettily faded version of the vivacious girl at her side, her sunny head poring over a complication of heathery threads.

Both looked up as Helen entered; straightened, and rubbed their backs with exclamations of greeting and surprise at how the time had flown. And Helen stepped over baskets and sidled round easels, careful lest she spill a drop on the fabric pooling from the sewing machine, or inadvertently knocked over a carton of woollen skeins.

'Just what the doctor ordered!' exclaimed Mrs West-cott with more thankfulness than originality, wrapping her thin hands about her brimming mug. 'Have you had a good day, Helen dear? Nothing too horrid, I hope.' She could never get over the novelty of having *three* daughters all dedicated to careers in nursing. Considering they had such a squeamish mother, it was nothing short of a miracle that her girls had turned out so useful and capable. (They got that from their father, of course. It was a myth about all clergy being unworldly and impractical people. That was their *wives* . . .) Margot Westcott smiled lovingly at dear Jenni. Jenni, of course, was a little bit different from the other two; a little bit of a dreamer by nature. It was somehow difficult to visualise her in a nurse's uniform . . . more of an Art School smock, she had always thought, judging by the child's very creative bent. Still, she sighed a soft gusty little sigh, you couldn't organise your children's lives for them; and there were depths in Jenni no one dreamed of; such a secretive, romantic child . . .

And Hannah; clever Hannah, who had once told her headmistress, no! she most definitely would not consider medicine instead of nursing. And nothing anyone could do or say had made Hannah change her mind. She had insisted on leaving after one year in the sixth-form, because that way she could start nursing at seventeen, as a pre-nursing student in the orthopaedic hospital where shortly she would be taking her Orthopaedics Diploma before transferring to the Royal Hanoverian where Helen had trained for state registration. Margot sipped her tea thoughtfully. Headstrong Hannah. Stubborn and gallant and full of courage . . .

Helen was telling them about her day, a censored version with the bits about Bram Markland considerately expurgated so her parents shouldn't worry. She was a good head taller than her two listeners, almost as

tall as LBW himself. Corn-blonde and blue-eyed, where
Jenni was a dainty freckled hazel-eyed snippet, her hair
a glorious riot of rich copper-gold curls. She always
looked as though the sun shone permanently on her
angelic, innocent head, a head that should never have to
contain the melancholy thoughts reflected now in those
wistful hazel eyes . . .

Helen was always quick to notice when something was
wrong. That was a strange look in Jenni's eyes; something was troubling little sister. She resolved to make an
opportunity for the younger girl to talk in quiet confidence, if she should feel the need. It was probably to do
with that Biology O Level resit she was working for,
after failing the exam the previous summer. It had been
decided to let a whole year pass, and then take the exam
again. Biology, or a science, was vital for nurse-training
at the Royal Hanoverian. Without it, Jenni was unlikely
to get in.

'I did put that casserole in the oven, didn't I, Helen?'
her mother was asking, interrupting the reverie over
Jenni's problems. 'You know what I am. It was the
Working Party in the church hall this afternoon, and I
think I saw to the casserole before I left the house . . .'
She hung her smock on a hook behind the door and
looked at Helen with a worried little frown.

'You did, mother dear, you did. I say . . .' Helen was
looking at a charcoal study of Jenni pinned up on an
easel. 'I like this, why don't you finish it?'

'She doesn't like my chin,' explained Jenni, standing
beside the drawing and sticking her chin out.

'I've made her too pretty,' said Mrs Westcott consideringly.

'Gee, thanks a bundle!' Jenni rolled her eyes until
they crossed above her nose. It was an infuriating trick

that never failed to upset the parents.

'Please don't do that, Jenni darling,' said her mother automatically. 'I haven't captured that Westcott chin—you've all inherited it from your father. Pointed chin on squarish jaw. It's very interesting. Sign of great character . . .'

'Determined!' declaimed Jenni.

'Huh, stubborn,' snorted Helen. 'Look at some of the tricks Hannah's got up to in the past.'

'Ah, that reminds me.' Margot Westcott dived a hand into the pocket of her discarded smock. 'Hannah's latest letter.'

'I want it first!' Jenni grabbed the envelope from her mother's outstretched hand. 'Can't wait for the next instalment of the saga of Dr Derby. I bet he's an absolute hunk.'

The three of them clattered down the bare wooden stairs that had once led up to the servants' quarters. Carpet was reserved for the rather grand main staircase, leading up from a rather grand hall. 'Daddy and I,' Margot was saying, 'would prefer to hear more about the work Hannah is supposedly doing at the Ortho-paedic Centre, rather than details of her numerous boyfriends.'

'Never mind,' Helen said comfortingly. 'In September she'll have finished that pre-nursing course and be joining the PTS at the Royal Hanoverian in London. Dr Derby will be out of sight and out of mind. Now let's get the table laid 'cos I for one am starving.'

Humming a contented little tune she bustled back and forth between kitchen and dining room. A place for Dad, and another for Mum; Jenni here, and Paul over here beside her. A ripple of pleasure ran down her spine at the thought that she'd be seeing her fiancé again in the next quarter of an hour, when he came in for his supper before Youth Club. She hadn't seen him for almost . . . twelve hours! To think whole months had gone by when she was nursing in London. And they had both survived the separation.

'You going to TCYC tonight?' she called to Jenni. 'I'm doing a First Aid demo and I need a willing patient.'

'I always go,' said Jenni in a strange little voice. Funny thought Helen. I get the strong impression that young lady would rather I stopped at home and did my knitting. Still, she shrugged at old memories, it's a difficult age, seventeen. I remember the days when I felt moody and cantankerous for no good reason.

Paul lived at the top of the vicarage in a flat converted from the attic rooms. Helen usually joined him for a bedtime cup of cocoa after Paul had been for his ten-minute jog; he liked to start and end the day with exercise.

He came in from his late-nigh. jog that evening all healthy and wide-awake and glowing. Stripped away his tracksuit top to reveal a white singlet which clung damply to his golden skin. Muscles rippled in his broad strong shoulders and the flesh of his arms and thighs was hard-packed and solid. In a tracksuit he looked every inch an athlete, and virile as they come. In a cassock, he was awesome.

Helen had heard his voice on the stairs below, calling a benevolent 'Good night to you too!' 'Who was that?' she asked curiously. 'Surely not Jenni? She should have been asleep long ago. Why, it's gone eleven.'

'She's such a sweet kid. She calls good night to me every evening—if she's still awake,' he added hurriedly, not wanting to get young Jenni into a row for staying awake after hours.

Helen looked a bit surprised, but refrained from commenting on this. Dad was strict about bedtime for schoolgirls and Jenni would get chewed off a strip if he found out. You'd think she'd have learned a lesson from Hannah's example.

She remembered about the 'if you can't beat 'em, join 'em' principle and informed Paul of her intention to join him for an early jogging session next morning. 'So knock on my door if I oversleep. My cardiovascular system could do with a bit of stress.'

'Get alongside me, then!' grunted Paul, 'Forty-five, forty-six, forty-seven . . .' He was face down on the carpet doing press-ups. Helen did as she was told, collapsing after six into a fit of giggles. She grabbed Paul round the middle, heaving his bulk over beside her and ruining his rhythm. 'You wretch!' he growled, 'I'll get you for that!'

Slender fingers located his ribs and dug in unmercifully. 'Don't you call me a wretch, you hulking brute you. I know where you're extremely ticklish and I have you at my mercy!'

After five minutes of horseplay they rolled onto their backs gasping and hysterical. Helen scrambled up and dusted herself down. 'Look at my jeans! Don't you ever do any cleaning up here?'

Paul was supposed to be responsible for his bed-sitter at the top of the vicarage. 'Your dear sister Hannah used to do it for me. Since she's gone off to do her orthopaedics diploma I can't say I've been too thorough.'

Helen looked amazed. 'Hannah! Doing your cleaning? That's a turn up for the books. She could never even keep her own bedroom tidy.' She filled the kettle from the tap in Paul's icy bathroom, shivering at being away from his hissing gas fire; carried it back in and plugged it into the socket.

'Never mind,' said Paul with casual certainty. 'Now you're back you'll do it for me, won't you, darling.'

Hands on hips, Helen glared mock-angrily down into his smiling face as he sat there cross-legged on the floor. 'It will be good experience for you—for when we're married and you've got a socking great place like this to look after,' he added winningly, with one of those endearing smiles that could melt the hardest heart. She collapsed again into his arms and it was five minutes before either of them noticed the kettle had filled the room with steam. It was Paul who got up and made their drinks while Helen curled up in a corner of the faded brown velvet sofa and watched his every move with dreamy eyes.

'When *are* we going to get married, darling? You said we should wait and see what the Bishop offers you this year—but now I'm home there seems no good reason to wait.'

He ran a broad hand through the tangle of his soft golden curls and seemed to be lost in thought. Then he carried their cocoa across the room and settled down with a comforting arm around the girl's slim shoulders, his fingers caressing the delicate bones beneath the cream angora sweater. Why don't you answer me? wondered Helen with a flash of irritation. You say you love me—but you seem so reluctant to name the day. You evade the question every time I summon up the courage to raise the subject.

'There really is no rush,' he said finally. 'You're only twenty-two and I'm twenty-eight. Many priests don't marry until their thirties. It's not as if I've a roof to put over your head, darling. I thought we'd agreed it was best to wait until my curacy is completed here. Which should be this year, if your father and the Bishop think I'm ready.'

'Most parishes prefer a married man,' Helen pointed out, her troubled eyes echoing her frustration. 'I still don't see why we can't marry now—there's plenty of room for us to live here. Besides,' she glanced teasingly up from under lowered lashes, 'it seems silly for us to be going to bed in separate rooms. I want us to share a double bed . . . don't you, Paul?'

His answer was to nibble her ear and whisper into the soft skin of her neck—which only made Helen sit up and pull away from him, giggling at what he had suggested. 'I know my parents are pretty broad-minded people, but not where their daughters' sleeping arrangements are concerned. "Not under my roof, you won't!"' she quoted, mimicking LBW at his most pontifical.

Her eyes gleamed as she remembered something else. 'Did you know all the nurses fancy you up at St Leonard's?'

Paul looked extremely interested, exaggerating his response just so as to be particularly annoying.

'All of them? Even that black-eyed beauty on Intensive Care? Hmmm . . .'

'Oh no,' Helen informed him loftily. 'Sorry, that was a small magnification of the facts. Only *half* the nurses. Every one else is madly in love with Bram Markland. You know, Bram Markland—the senior man on Casualty. I was working with him today. He's . . . he's definitely a fascinating man.' And that's not the biggest lie I've ever told, she thought with a shiver. But it's so far from the truth that it's *nearly* the biggest. That one was when I told Dad my new coat cost half what it did!

Paul tucked his hands behind his head and stretched

out his long muscular legs. 'I'm pretty well acquainted with Bram Markland. He's quite a buddy of mine in a funny sort of way. Yes, I do believe I'd heard he was something of a heart-throb. And you say you find him fascinating, do you young woman? Well, just come over here and say that to my face.'

'No no—I'm going downstairs now. I need my beauty sleep.' Small shrieks and splutters of laughter filled the air, as Paul demonstrated what he thought of his fiancée's assertion about her feelings for Bram Markland. 'Ow no, truly Paul—I don't like him at all. And he hates the sight of me. Truly. Truly!' Released, Helen threw back the wild mass of her hair and clasped her hot cheeks as she rocked, laughing, on her heels.

Paul thought she looked pretty as a picture, and said so. He also said it would be impossible for anyone to hate the sight of her. 'More likely he couldn't take his eyes off your enchanting face,' he insisted. 'I've seen Bram, his eyes trailing some young student nurse while he's supposed to be stitching my broken head.'

'What do you mean,' asked Helen curiously, 'when you say Bram's a buddy of yours in a "funny" sort of way.'

'Oh, you know. We meet around the hospital, eye each other with suspicion. He reads me lectures about warm-up exercises when I get carted up to Casualty on a Saturday afternoon to have my war wounds patched. Darling—*why* are we discussing Bram Markland like this? You need your beauty sleep and so do I. I'm taking the early service tomorrow on LBW's day off.'

Immediately Helen looked contrite. She ran an apologetic hand over Paul's enviable biceps, considering how a bit of muscle would do wonders for the lanky Markland. Heaven be praised for her two days off. She was on the point of pressing her fiancé into an explanation of the sort of lectures someone so supremely unfit could deliver to the like of Paul, but decided that must wait for a more reasonable hour of the day. There would be plenty of time over the next forty-eight hours.

Late as it was, Jenni's light was still glowing under her bedroom door. Helen knocked and peeped in, to find the youngster sitting up in bed among a confusion of books and papers spread across the pink candlewick coverlet. 'You should be asleep, Jenni. What's all this then?'

'Blasted biology! Bilious-making biology. Oh blow the biology.'

Helen flopped onto the bed. 'You need it if you want to nurse. Besides, if you don't like biology what makes you think you'll enjoy the theoretical side of nursing?'

'I just know it. I'm fine on the *human* biol—but some of this is more chemistry than anything. And I loathe all the plant stuff.'

'I agree it's not an easy science, though people tend to believe otherwise. Why didn't you choose Human Biology when you were picking your O-Level options? That's the one I took.'

'And not be able to take Geography? One of my best subjects? I got grade A—and I'm doing it for A-Level.' Jenni rubbed her nose with a childlike fist.

Helen, flicking through her exercise books, looked up and smiled. 'Your work is beautifully drawn—and I've never seen such immaculate notes. Are you quite sure you don't want to go to Art School after all?'

Hazel eyes rolled up to heaven in exasperation. 'For the hundredth time, sister dear, I want to nurse. I have always wanted to nurse. Try and stop me.'

'You could be a medical artist . . . No, well, perhaps not. Anyway the exam's not until June, is it. No need to be working at this hour of the night.'

'I've failed Biology once already! If I plough it this time the Royal Hanoverian won't look at me—even if you were the Gold Medallist last year! No London school of nursing will want me without a science pass. I've written to all the top schools. "Get a science dear, then contact us again." I've only got this interview because you're the bee's knees with Miss Sugden, the Director of Nurse Education.'

Helen frowned consideringly. 'It *is* more difficult to get into nursing. Everyone must have five GCE passes now for SRN, and even that's not enough when the hospitals have so many more applicants than there are places available for training. You're right to be doing Advanced Levels.'

Jenni's face was so despondent that Helen's kind heart longed to cheer her up. Everyone seemed a bit down tonight—except Paul. He always looked on the bright side. She stretched out a hand and ruffled the rich shiny curls. 'You've got six O Levels already, and you're working for three Advanced Levels. That's good enough for any nurse.' Jennie's mouth opened to interrupt, but Helen insisted on finishing what she was saying. 'Hush up and listen. Now I'm home I shall coach you for the re-sit. You'll pass—I'll eat my old school panama if you don't. Ugh! What a thought. It never looked the same after I dropped it in the canal . . .'

Jenni looked up from under her lashes, the corners of her mouth dimpling. 'Can I hold you to that?' she said mischievously.

'You horror, I bet you would. And anyway, it's not the end of the world if you train at a provincial school.

London streets by night are not the safest. And SRN training is the same standard wherever you go. I've met nurses who tell me it's a positive advantage to train where there isn't a medical school attached to the hospital. The nurses learn to do all the jobs that medical students would handle on the wards. You can come out of some of the top hospitals and not know how to take blood, for instance.' I'm protesting too much, thought Helen. If I go on like this she'll be convinced I think she won't pass. Still, it's true enough there's a myth about London training that needs quashing for good and all.

'Now promise me you'll put that light out and go to sleep.'

Obediently Jenni swept her papers into a pile and dropped them on the carpet. 'Leave the door open a bit,' she said, yawning.

Helen smiled to herself as she did as she was asked, crossing the landing to go to her own room. Little sister afraid of the dark.

But Jenni had long outgrown that particular fear. Something very different was concerning her. She lay with her eyes on the door to Helen's bedroom, checking that she went back there after she had been to the bathroom. Checking that she didn't go near the stairs that led upward to Paul in the attic above.

A hot little tear trickled from the corner of one hazel eye, dampening a coppery curl and the cotton pillowslip. Until Helen came back, Jenni had had Paul all to herself; and she could hardly bear to think that one day he was going to marry her sister and go away from there for ever. Of course Paul didn't know how she felt about him. And neither did anyone else in all the world. Not even her best friends at school . . .

For it was Jenni Westcott's most closely guarded secret. She was madly in love with her sister's fiancé, despairingly in love with Father Paul.

CHAPTER THREE

'WHICH CUBICLE, Staff?' The ambulance attendants waited as Helen checked the treatment area with an appraising eye.

'Number six, if you please.' She held back the curtain while the two men lowered the teenager onto the couch. The girl was alert and in obvious pain, her clothes soaked in blood and the cuts and grazes on her face and hands and limbs gritty with dirt and gravel.

'Details?' Helen heard Bram Markland's deep voice just outside the cubicle. Then, 'Yes, I see . . . did the driver stop, or what? . . . I should think so too.'

There was a swish of fabric and he was standing next to her in the confines of the cubicle, his eyes barely acknowledging that she was there, his attention all on the injured girl. Once more I'm the invisible woman, Helen thought ironically. Oh well, I should complain—it cuts the hassle . . .

A quick examination seemed to have satisfied the doctor. He said very little, though Helen saw him give the girl a comforting broad wink. Blood was running down from the side of her mouth and settling in the crevices of her neck. Gently the doctor lifted her top lip with his thumb, pulled back the lower lip to examine her bottom jaw.

'Good, good. Teeth all present and correct. No bones broken, Sal. We'll tidy you up and put in a few stitches here and there. Keep you in overnight—and in a day or so you'll feel good as new.'

She tried to smile at him, but it clearly hurt her mouth to make the effort. 'I'm not Sal—I—I'm Felicity. I was . . . going to my music lesson. Do you think they picked up my music case?'

'It's here love,' said Bram. 'Hadn't got your piano with you, I hope. I'm not much of an expert when it comes to patching up pianos.' Even Helen had to smile at this. Bram certainly had the knack of calming youngsters. She could just imagine Jenni— not much older than Felicity here—falling under his spell. She glanced down as he turned towards her, hiding from him her appreciation of his bedside manner as he issued instructions for this patient's treatment.

Then . . . Oh no! Not again, I simply don't believe this. It's too much, he's doing it deliberately. One sock navy, the other a bilious shade of sage green. Helen knew her mouth was gaping foolishly, closed it with an effort, and concentrated on Bram's upper torso, her nose level with a glaring concoction of bright yellow, green and sky-blue tie . . .

What you need is a wife, Dr Markland. (Heaven help the poor woman!) She'd never let you leave the house looking like that.

Cool, watchful eyes were reading the staff nurse's expressive face, the corner of that lop-sided mouth lifting in a smirk of mockery at her evident disapproval. Then the casualty officer was issuing instructions for Felicity to be transferred to the clean theatre, where her superficial cuts and bruises would be attended to. Helen followed him meekly out of the cubicle, respecting the doctor where she found it hard to respect the man. 'There's no shock syndrome and she's alert and reasonably coherent. I'll take another look when you've got her into theatre—but I'm quite certain there's no internal injury.'

Helen wondered how he could bring himself to be so confident before seeing the evidence of the X-ray plates; but typically there was no hesitation in his diagnosis, clear and confident as she had now learned to expect.

The Accident and Emergency Department of St Leonard's had three theatres—one large, and two smaller theatres designated 'clean' and 'dirty'. High-grade bacterial infections were dealt with in the 'dirty' theatre, suspect wounds cleansed and irrigated and stitched, boils lanced and patients with urine retention catheterised. The clean theatre on the other hand dealt with minor surgical procedures that must be carried out under aseptic conditions. To this one Felicity was transferred, and Helen with the help of a senior student, a bouncy red-cheeked lass called Ronnie, managed gently to ease away the blood-stained clothing without having to damage any of it by cutting. 'That's a good tweed coat,' said Helen. 'Dry-cleaned, it will come up like new. I'm glad we haven't had to take the scissors to it.'

Patiently the two nurses bent over the girl, their gloved fingers using swabs and forceps to capture the grit and bits of dirt and ease them out of the cuts and grazes. Felicity had been struck by the car and thrown yards distant; but she hadn't hit anything and her injuries were not grave. They were, all the same, nasty and painful.

Bram came sauntering in. Felicity was giving little cries and whimpers and Helen was making soothing murmurs to her as she worked, just as she might to a baby. 'There, there. You're being *so* brave. There, there—such a good girl you are.'

The two nurses stepped back out of Bram's way. He looked at the extensive bruising, the skin smudged with dirt and discolouration. Looked and nodded. He too murmured reassuringly as his hands moved searchingly over the rib cage, feeling for any misalignment or special area of tenderness. His eyes never left his patient's face—as was customary when examining the chest, so that if his fingers should discover any torn muscle or cracked rib he might not cause unnecessary suffering.

Watching him, Helen was struck by the fact that one could almost believe he really cared; that his face could so reflect concern and sympathy—quite out of character with its normal expression of scornful arrogance. He didn't care, of course. It would drain a man of every emotional resource if he let every case get to him. And Bram's emotions were few—and basic. Still, he made the effort to look as if he understood what Felicity was going through. And Helen must applaud him for that.

The diagnosis was delivered with Bram's customary laconic confidence. 'No other injuries—just as I expected. I'll leave you to it.' And tossing his gloves into the bin he strolled out of the theatre.

Over a snatched coffee in Sister Guppy's office, Helen let curiosity get the better of her discretion. Why couldn't she get the blasted man out of her thoughts? 'Bram Markland strikes me as pretty experienced,' she observed casually. 'What's his background, Sister?'

For some strange reason Elsie Guppy looked almost furtive. A little crease furrowed Helen's eyebrows as she realised Sister was avoiding any comment on Bram's private life. 'Very experienced,' she emphasised, recalling that he had worked in several other hospitals before coming to St Leonard's A & E department. 'I shouldn't be at all surprised to see him moving on up the ladder towards a consultancy before long. He's working for his Fellowship, of course. And though he's got an obvious flair for casualty work, rumour has it that his old hospital is trying to tempt him back to London with a teaching post.'

Helen's mug froze in mid-air. Might she then soon be rid of this disturbing man who was taking up far too much of her thoughts and attention? 'Where is that?'

Sister's reply had her mopping at coffee splashes on her pristine grey dress. But that was a top-ranking hospital! Stricter even than the Royal Hanoverian . . . and to think they were angling to get Bram Markland back, horrible socks and all.

'Then they must think very highly of him,' she remarked tartly. 'Do you think they'll take him away from us soon?'

Sister Guppy took that question at face value, looking quite crestfallen at the prospect of losing Bram. 'Keep that to yourself, Helen dear. Perhaps I shouldn't have spoken as I did. Not just yet,' she crossed her fingers with a silent prayer, 'hopefully anyway. He's so able, Helen. This remarkable talent for making clear and unambiguous diagnoses—so important in Casualty work.'

'He certainly is pretty sure of himself!' Helen's generous mouth tightened at certain memories that still niggled. She collected the mugs and rinsed them rapidly in the small sink. 'Now, you wanted to give that first-year student a tutorial. Shall I send her in to you?'

Sister consulted a list on her notice board. 'That's right, Emma Hedge. Bright little girl—reminds me of you when—'

'When I was young and still full of illusions. Sister Guppy Mark Two, I thought I was going to be! Now it seems I'll be giving it all up for love and marriage.'

'But a vicar's wife can keep on with her work. Lots do.'

'They have to, unless they're particularly fond of living in poverty.' Helen bit her lip. 'I know I'm young, but I did think we might start a family pretty soon . . .'

At that moment Bram walked in, heard what she was saying and looked at Helen as though she had crawled out of a hole. 'What do we train these girls for?' he threw out, the scornful tone of his voice crushing her mercilessly. 'All they want is to be baby machines, the little idiots.'

Helen did not wait to hear more, too stunned to have the wit to stand up for her dreams and aspirations. She sought out Emma, then charged into the first treatment room and began slamming equipment into place until her system had regained its usual calm, her one ray of sunshine the revelation that Bram Markland would be quitting St Leonard's in the foreseeable future.

All afternoon Helen worked with the junior casualty officer, Charlie Robards, a jovial character with his teasing banter and his spotted bow ties. Dr Markland had gone to a meeting in the admin. block.

Casualty seemed so pleasant now; Helen found the atmosphere relaxed and unfraught, in spite of the steady flow of traffic that meant they could never let up for a moment. She found herself wondering why no one else commented on how nice it was not to have Bram Markland prowling around like a sabre-toothed tiger, appraising the scene with those cool dispassionate eyes . . .

He definitely did not like her. Sister Guppy must have seen it now, for herself.

As far as I'm concerned, Helen informed Dr Mark-

land in her imagination, while concentrating on the
delicate task of shaving a very hairy pre-operative leg; as
far as *I'm* concerned you can go back to London tomorrow. I shan't miss you, not one little bit. Even though
you may be a first-rate doctor, according to Guppy's
gospel. 'Hold still, there's a dear, Mr Colvin. No, I'm
not likely to take your leg off—not so long as you keep it
just like that. Very still.'

Oh, and Dr Markland, please do be sure to pack all
your horrible socks when you go. I bet they're made of
nylon . . .

Pop music reverberated its pounding beat, a group of
teenagers dancing in rapt concentration close by the
amplifier. Several boys were playing chess, apparently
oblivious of the noise around their tables; Paul, in jeans,
shirt-sleeves rolled up for action, was letting an eager
youth thrash him at table-tennis, and Jenni sat gloomily
on a stool while her friend Sarah dealt with an imaginary
wound on the top of her skull.

Across the Church Hall Helen caught Paul's eye and
winked.

Under her supervision some of the girls were busily
occupied in constructing ring pads out of triangular
bandages, pleased as punch to find it less complicated
than it looked. 'Hey, Miss, this is really easy when you
know how!'

'I'll give you "Miss",' teased Helen, rumpling the
speaker's enthusiastic head. 'You're not in school now—
and I'm Helen. You are a clever lot, you pick things up
so fast.' She was quite unconscious of the fact that she
was a born teacher and her first-aiders were hanging
breathlessly upon her every word. All but one, who was
determined not to succumb . . . 'Now can anyone re-

mind me why we're putting this ring pad on Jenni's head and not just covering the wound with a thick gauze dressing?'

'Cause you want me to look a right twit!' grumbled the reluctant 'patient', hunching her neck into her shoulders and glowering at her sister.

'Someone else can be the model next time,' said Helen reasonably. 'But what else is complicating Jenni's skull fracture?'

'There's a foreign body sticking out of it!' came the chorused answer. 'Piece of glass—or some bone,' added Sarah. 'We put a piece of gauze very gently over to cover the foreign body, then the ring pad goes round it to put pressure on the bleeding . . .'

'Without pushing the bit of bone back in,' finished off another voice.

'Ah, but how are you going to keep the pad in place without bandaging over the foreign body?' Helen looked round her little group, smiling at the frowning faces and chewing lips. 'What a problem, eh? Now watch very carefully while I demonstrate this. It's a bit tricky and I'm going to need another of those triangular bandages. But this is what you're all going to practise on each other.'

Once she was mercifully released, Jenni shot off in the direction of the cloakroom to comb her hair and adjust her make-up. Helen covered up a surreptitious smile; there must be some new Galahad around whom she hadn't yet heard of. Who might it be . . . that tall dark-eyed boy over there with the brooding good-looks? Or that fair chap with the ear-ring, good heavens— wasn't it the organist's son, Richard Brandish? How he'd changed from the angelic little choir boy Helen remembered, reading comics under the choir stalls during the sermon . . . Jenni and her quick-change boyfriends!

She dragged her attention back to the bandaging that was causing a certain amount of hilarity among the onlookers. Paul appeared at her side. 'What a sight! Wish I had my camera with me,' he chortled.

'Give them a chance—they're doing this for the first time. And stop laughing, or my first-aid class will die the death. Jenni's fed up with me, but then she's already done the St John's Ambulance First Aid certificate, which is far superior to my own poor efforts.' Helen stood on tiptoe and smoothed the damp curls off her fiancé's forehead. From the door of the cloakroom Jenni watched in silence, then turned back and disappeared.

'Poor darling, you're in a muck sweat,' teased Helen in a low murmur so no one could hear. 'It was nice of you to let Jamie win the table-tennis game. I saw what you were doing.' Her fingers rested for a moment against his damp cotton shirt. 'When the girls have finished I'll make you a nice cold drink of squash. Ah, here's Jen. Jen, be a love and make Paul a drink, will you?'

Jenni nodded and was back in two ticks. 'Thanks gorgeous,' said Paul, giving her a hearty hug. 'Loved that hat you were wearing just now.' Jenni went painfully pink but made no move to break out of his grasp. But she tossed her sunny head and hissed at Helen, 'I told you you were showing me up!'

'Be off with you,' scolded Paul, sending little sister away with a playful pat on the rump. The two of them watched her saunter into the crowd of dancers and begin swinging her body about in a self-conscious way that suggested she knew admiring eyes were upon her. 'You mustn't tease her, darling. Looks are so important at that age.'

'Mark my words, she'll be a heartbreaker one day.' Paul sounded thoughtful, his gaze still on Jenni's slender figure in skintight red velvet jeans. 'She's like a Dickens heroine. Innocent little face, skin like a speckled flower petal—and that lovely rich hair . . .'

'Steady on,' protested Helen in mock alarm. 'I might get jealous.' Then, thoughtfully, 'Dad always says Jenni looks just like Mum did when she was young. Mum must have been lovely.'

'She still is—you all are, what an incredible family. Even the cat's good-looking! Now I must zoom off and sort out the Chess ladder, while you count your bandages back in.'

It was only towards the end of Club Night that Helen suddenly found an inkling of what might be going on in little sister's mind. The music had been switched off and Paul was up on the stage talking to the whole club gathered there at his feet. He looked wonderful; every inch of him strong and vital, his legs muscularly outlined by tight faded denims, sinewy arms thrusting out of rolled-up shirt sleeves, knuckles digging into his hipbones.

'Valentine's Day!' he was reminding them. 'I want a volunteer committee to help me organise some frantics for Club Night that week.' 'Frantics' was a Paul-coined word he'd conjured up for fun-and-games at Youth Club on special occasions. 'Who's going to help?'

Helen clapped her hands over her ears at the hullabaloo that sixty healthy young throats could produce. Her head swivelled as she searched out Jenni to exchange a complicit grin; but the smile turned to uncertainty as she failed to catch her sister's eye. The girl was intent on Paul, her defences down. The look of adoration on her rapt face was so obviously devoted that Helen groaned inside. Paul, teasing, cajoling and bantering, towering above the throng. Jenni, poor Jenni, her eyes glued to his laughing boyish face and that virile athletic frame; her heart on her sleeve for anyone to see.

Helen turned away, pale and troubled. It all came together now; the suspicion of hostility, Jenni's refusal to open up to the sister who had once been her confidante . . . the poor poor kid. She must be so unhappy inside. And trust dear old Paul to have noticed nothing. It would never occur to him that Jenni might regard him as anything other than the brother she never had, which was exactly how he behaved towards her. It would need all Helen's kindness and sensitivity to help Jenni get over this one; but help she must, before someone got badly hurt. And with a shiver as she recalled her fiancé's admiring observation on the subject of her youngest sister, Helen felt suddenly none too sure of herself or her own place in Paul's generous heart . . .

Next morning Helen woke with it all sorted out in her mind. She had lain awake, staring into the darkness, searching her conscience to find a solution to the problems that had reared up since her return from London. It was no good telling yourself that perhaps you'd done the wrong thing, coming back home and taking the job at St Leonard's, she thought.

One, I resolve not to badger Paul any more about fixing a date for our wedding. Two, I will be extra kind to Jenni, give her lots of help with her Biology exam—even if I'm weary to the back teeth after a bad day coping with Bram Markland. What's more I'll do my utmost to take her mind off Paul—God knows how, but between us we'll come up with something. And as for Bram Markland . . .

Helen lay there frowning. Five minutes until she must be up for her early morning jog with Paul. Five minutes to think about Bram Markland. If only he wasn't so—so strangely fascinating in his horrible way. If he was incompetent, as well as nasty and unkempt, then you could just do your own work as well as possible and dismiss him from your thoughts when you weren't near him. Out of sight, out of mind. The trouble was, on the rare occasions the beastly fellow smiled . . . it was altogether devastatingly attractive.

And an engaged person has no business noticing such things, Helen chided herself severely. The trouble with you, my girl, is you've been foolish enough to let the gossip about Bram's legendary activities get fixed into your silly little brain. And your feelings are hurt because he doesn't like you at all.

She swung her legs out of bed, wincing as her toes met the cold lino, padded over to the dressing-table and with her head flung down towards her knees began a vigorous attack in brushing the night-time tangles out of her long blonde tresses.

With the rush of blood to the brain came the solution. Helen straightened up and stared at herself in the mirror. Of course, it was perfectly straightforward. Do as you would be done by. Be kind and courteous and pleasant, whatever his mood . . .

Trouble is, mused she, a hairgrip clamped between her teeth as she hoisted her thick hair up into a convenient ponytail; though I've been brought up to believe you should turn the other cheek when someone strikes you—and I'm fairly placid by nature (I hate rows and bad-feeling)—something about Bram Markland makes me want to challenge the man, not let him trample all over me, or anyone else for that matter . . . gosh, is that the time? Paul will be raring to go.

While Helen was tearing into her tracksuit Sister Guppy was coming out of Holy Trinity Church, treading cautiously on the frosty steps. 'Don't want to be carried feet-first into my own department!'

- 'Indeed not!' LBW lent a steadying hand to elderly Mrs Harper whose arthritis was not improved by the February early-morning chill. She did well, poor soul, to get out at all, let alone drag herself to the Thursday seven a.m. service. 'Takes me hours to get dressed, Vicar,' she informed him breathlessly. 'Do you know I was up at half-five. Well, I mean it's nothing to me. When I was in service at the Old Hall . . .'

Sister fumbled in her pocket for the car keys. Wouldn't be time for egg-and-bacon today—Thursdays was muesli and coffee for she never missed early church. It was the day her parents had died together in a car crash, seven years back. And she had lived alone ever since, no one seeming in a hurry to marry her.

She was opening the car door when Paul came jogging past, his black cassock exchanged for tracksuit and trainers, Helen chugging along in his wake, their breath streaming in thin white clouds behind them. As he passed, Paul reached out and clapped the nurse across the shoulders. 'Nice to see you, Guppy dear!' he panted as he passed by, never noticing how his hearty gesture almost threw the small wiry figure across the front seats.

'Paul!' admonished Helen in concern. 'Look what you've done to poor Guppy. Are you all right? . . . That man doesn't know his own strength!' But Paul was already disappearing into the mists ahead.

'What's he doing then—training for the London Marathon at Easter?' Elsie settled her beige felt over her eyebrows and surveyed Helen's emerald jogging suit.

Very nice, but not for the mature. Helen, dear girl, would look pretty in a dustbin liner.

Helen looked surprised. 'Is that mind-reading or just an educated guess? You're dead right—it's Paul's latest brainwave to raise money for church funds. He wants everyone to sponsor him for the whole twenty-six miles. I'm just joining in the practice for the sheer joy of it.' She dropped her shoulders and panted in mock-exhaustion.

'No doubt we shall be given the gory details at next week's PCC meeting, and expected to canvas every house in the parish.'

'Oh I expect so,' agreed Helen happily. 'I'm so proud of him. We'll saturate the hospital with sponsorship forms and get everyone involved.'

'I wonder what your young man will come up with next?' Elsie Guppy raised a comical eyebrow. 'Floodlit rugby in the churchyard, perhaps? Abseiling down the tower?'

Helen grabbed her shoulder in horror. 'Sounds just up Paul's street—promise me you'll never suggest it to him! I must be off—he's way out of sight now. See you after breakfast. Byeee.'

And an hour later she was walking round the quiet department with a nice cup of tea, easing herself into the start of the routine day. The night staff had gone, handing over their report and leaving everything neat and tidy. Helen was just checking. On Casualty it was futile to try and predict the slow or the busy times. At any given moment the breakfast-time lull might be disrupted. It depended on how many mums managed to slice into themselves as well as the loaf of bread; how many dads tried to take it too fast to work on the slippery roads. How many school children were careless on the snail-trail to the local comprehensive . . .

All the same, these considerations apart, Helen was humming a contented little tune—which died a sudden death, as coming out of the plaster room she collided with Dr Markland. Late on duty and struggling with his white coat as if it had a mind and will of its own.

'Good morning, Doctor!' said Helen brightly and with admirable recall of her good intentions. You've just trodden on my foot but I'm in a forgiving mood. 'Do let me give you a hand. I think your left sleeve is inside out. If I can just take that for a moment—'

Bram slouched against the wall as if he couldn't rely on his legs for any support in the matter. Without obvious expression of gratitude, he allowed himself to be re-coated. 'I feel bloody terrible.'

Helen frowned when he swore and tried not to feel insulted that he should feel free to do so in front of her. 'You look frightful,' she agreed. I knew I was right— your eyes *are* naturally red. 'What do you think is the matter with you?' To jump to ready-made conclusions would be unkind—and anyway it's not a nurse's job to diagnose, she reminded herself while an irresistible smirk tugged at the corners of her humorous mouth. Fancy coming on duty in such a state.

Bram was mumbling something about 'no sleep' and 'headache' and 'flashing lights before the eyes'. It was no exaggeration—the man looked deathly. Helen tried to keep up a sympathetic expression, but *really*, how irresponsible considering that Dr Markland carried the weight of the department on his sagging shoulders. Perhaps . . . a sudden fear struck her. Perhaps he had a secret drink problem? All the stress and everything. Someone ought to try and help. Not her of course. He didn't like her, after all. But someone should be keeping an eye on him.

'Come with me into the sluice.' She put a solicitous hand on his arm, held the door wide open so he should not bump against the frame. 'That's right,' she pulled a stool invitingly out from beneath the sink, 'you rest here a moment.'

It was Bram's turn to feel mystified; like a spider being enticed into the fly's web, he worked out in his confused and throbbing brain. What was this cool blonde girl up to now? apparently sympathising with his—er—condition.

Now he was more alert—and all suspicion. How many were there of those sleek black legs, bustling about filling kettles and putting out mugs as Staff Nurse Westcott swished around the sluice with her handspan waist and spotless white apron. Eight legs was it? Female spider, trying to trap a surgeon far too fly to fall for 'nice' parsons' daughters yearning to save immortal souls.

Yes, deduced Bram with a frown of inspiration. That's her game—reformation of my character, that's what. And since I'm perfectly content the way I am, someone's going to be mighty disillusioned.

He concealed a wickedly shameless grin at the prospect of some goodly fun at Helen's expense, groaned dramatically and watched for the reaction out of the corner of one bleary eye . . .

CHAPTER FOUR

DOES THE man think I'm daft?

Helen poured out Bram's tea hot and strong, unimpressed by the standard of his performance. *Definitely* no loss to RADA. 'Feeling better? That's good,' she said, brisk and professional, no sympathy going to waste.

Bram looked as if his tea had been sweetened with carbolic. 'And now I'm supposed to have asbestos lips!' he snarled sarcastically. The woman was clearly a sadist, totally lacking in the gentler feminine qualities—in spite of all appearances to the contrary. Typical nurse. Bram began to wonder who was baiting whom . . .

'Sorry.' She took back the drink and added cold milk with the placid calm of one humouring a pettish infant. 'I had the idea you liked things hot and sweet.'

This earned Helen a sharply calculating stare, one that totally belied the heartrending performance of a man struggling in to work on his last legs. 'How comforting to know my preferences get such careful consideration.' The doctor hitched one lanky leg on to a higher rung of the stool, leaned back against the wall, regarding her with eyes like red-hot coals. 'I was beginning to fear you might turn out to be the one nurse I could never make a relationship with.'

Now it was Helen's turn to feel at a loss. Her skin prickled and her tongue tied itself up in knots. What on earth was he getting at? 'I er—I'm sure we shall continue to get along together, Dr Markland.'

Just then a genuine groan broke from Bram's tautened lips and his hand pressed involuntarily against his breastbone. Helen was across the yards that separated them in the space of seconds. She grabbed the mug before its sugary contents got split over the freshly polished floor. Mustn't have the cleaning staff upset, not at any price.

'Whatever were you drinking last night?' she questioned sternly. 'Whisky? Vodka? Was it champagne?'

'Champagne doesn't give you a hangover!' rasped Bram huskily. 'Well, how would I know about that?' said Helen tartly, her composure quite recovered. 'Us church mouses don't get much of the stuff. What was it then—the whisky?' You look like a whisky man, she thought. Not that *I'm* much of an expert. But we have to isolate the poison before we can make a start on the cure. If Bram's liver is to be saved, then someone must tread where angels fear to. And at least I shan't ruin a beautiful friendship.

The red eyes rolled. 'What *is* this then? The Spanish Inquisition?' He was fumbling in his pockets, coming up with a phial of white tablets, tossing a couple down his throat.

Helen gave him back his tea. 'Drink up. You know how important it is to swallow plenty of liquid with pills of any sort. They might stick in your gullet and do all kinds of damage.' There was a twinkle in the girl's eye but Bram was too intent on inspecting the contents of the mug to notice. Looking down on him Helen was aware of the hollowed cheeks and the lines that carved down his face, heightening that sardonic mien. Once she had thought he looked too thin for his lanky length, but for the first time she noticed that the thigh his hand rested on was as strong-looking as she remembered Paul's.

'What I really need is some hair of the dog,' he was muttering to himself. Tea and good advice (sympathy was clearly out of the question from this formidable young woman!)—what a merciless combination. 'I had good reason to celebrate last night. Finished a Paper I've been working on.'

'Strikes me you're always celebrating,' said Helen absentmindedly, not really listening. Was that the sound of an ambulance siren?

'And how would you know!' retorted Bram, a little hurt. She might have taken the trouble to offer a word or two of congratulation. Heartless wench.

Helen heard this and winced. It was a tough assignment she'd let herself in for, reforming the doctor's regrettable habits. But she couldn't back out at an early stage in so worthwhile a mission. Bram lifted his head and looked at her; a look so tired and vulnerable that Helen's fingers ached to stretch out and brush the hair out of his eyes—though of course she couldn't let them. She leaned over to collect the empty mugs and get cracking with the work that must be piling up for them both.

'Are those eyelashes dyed?' His warm breath fanned her cheeks and Helen leapt back in indignation.

'Dyed eyelashes indeed. Only fashion models would bother with that sort of thing!'

Bram looked knowledgeable. 'Not so. I've had several blonde girlfriends who dyed their lashes navy or charcoal.'

'Well you would, wouldn't you.' The legend of Dr Markland, thought Helen with a sigh.

Bram rose to his feet and stretched languidly. His eyes looked clearer already. Their real colour, discovered Helen as he towered over her, was not so much red as a velvety mahogany. She was beginning to understand why others fell for him. He wasn't horrible at all—not when you got to know him better. Little boy lost under that powerful façade.

'Amazing,' he was murmuring in that direct and un-abashed manner—so disconcerting to a girl who had been brought up not to make personal comments about other people. 'Such thick black lashes . . . with corn-flower eyes and skin like cream. I don't think I've ever had that combination.'

Helen's cheeks turned hot with indignation and all her kindly feelings quite disappeared. If he had got out a little black book and started detailing her specifications along with her phone number, she would not have been at all surprised. Useful subject matter for future refer-ence, should a free night crop up between those endless 'celebrations'. She stood rooted to the spot, like some petrified creature mindlessly fascinated by its predator.

Bram caught hold of her chin, revelling in her silent outrage and in having regained the upper hand. 'No lipstick either . . . girls who don't wear lipstick are hoping to be . . .' his mouth hovered consideringly above hers.

He's going to kiss me—how dare he! Helen was aghast, clutching to her throbbing apron front an armful of crockery. And me with not a free hand to defend myself. I can't bear to look!

. . . but suddenly her chin was free and her startled eyes snapped wide. Just in time to see the sluice door swivel-to on well-oiled hinges. To hear the departing careless whistle echo mockingly back at her as Bram strolled away down the passage.

From then on Helen was her usual model of efficiency, moving from one task to the next, with never a second to waste on fuelling the fire that simmered deep in the core of her being. The face she presented to the world was totally calm. As she worked alongside Dr Markland her hands betrayed not a tremor as their fingers exchanged instruments, case notes, blood samples, sometimes brushing skin to skin as casually as if there was not the least contention between them.

You couldn't fault him. He was as capable and confident as ever, in spite of the state in which he'd come on duty. Not that Helen wanted to witness any professional incompetence—heaven forbid! But how could a man burn the candle at both ends and keep up his usual high performance as senior casualty surgeon? It ought to require superhuman effort—yet Bram showed no sign of working under undue strain. 'Come on Andrew,' he was saying jovially to one of the dressers—senior medical students from the university's medical faculty, who were assigned to treat minor injuries in the Accident Unit. 'I'm going to show you a text-book blow-out fracture. Where d'you put my patient, Helen?'

'The eye-treatment cubicle is clear now, Doctor. She's in there waiting for you.'

Helen led the way, setting down the pile of buff folders she had been about to take to the office on a chair by the wash basin. The patient, a woman in her late twenties, had refused to say what had caused such a violent blow directly to her left eye. The assault had taken place at home, and it was Helen's compassionate conclusion that here they were dealing with a battered wife; too loyal—or too frightened—to land her husband in the soup.

Bram was steadying the patient's head with his fingers on her jaw. Unwelcome and total recall shivered through the staff nurse who swallowed hard as she observed the doctor's examination. Andrew, the dresser, leaned close, grateful that Dr Markland was taking such an interest in teaching him.

'You can't move that eye, can you?' Bram said. 'No, my dear, I don't want you to try. Breathe through your mouth—and above all don't blow your nose.' He took the trouble to explain why pressure from the nostrils might shift the damaged bone and tissue in the eye socket—and hence make matters worse, phrasing it so as not to frighten the woman unnecessarily. This was a facet of his work that never failed to impress the staff he worked with. People were much more likely to respond to a doctor who took time and trouble to explain things to them; the patients to be more helpful and co-operative; the staff to get greater satisfaction from the everyday routine.

Bram moved a yard or so away from the treatment couch and spoke quietly to Helen and Andrew. 'If I may use you as a demo model,' he said with exquisite politeness, grabbing hold of Helen's head and pulling off her cap. His hands enclosed her skull as, towering over her, he demonstrated how a violent punch or kick gives rise to a blow-out fracture. 'Thus if the patient can't move the eye it's an indication an ocular muscle has been trapped in the fracture.'

Andrew looked from Helen to Bram and back to Helen. Her mouth was tight with annoyance and her eyes blazed up at Bram. A stray wisp of hair fell across her nose and the surgeon with a smile and surprisingly gentle fingers tucked it away behind her ear. Andrew thought she looked terribly pretty—though cross. Perhaps Dr Markland had stood her up the night before, and was even now regretting it. That soft little gesture spoke of a wish to make amends.

The moment was as quickly past. Helen snatched back her cap and pinned it hastily into place. 'Nurse will put a cool pad over that eye,' Bram was telling the patient, 'then we'll get you up to a ward where a specialist can take a look at you.' With a smile of reassurance and a brief touch of the hand on hers, he moved on to the next case awaiting his attention.

'What a nice man,' murmured the woman.

'I can see to that for you, Helen,' offered Andrew. 'You've left a pile of records on the chair, I expect they're needed somewhere.'

'Wh-what?' For a moment Helen was uncharacteristically vague, as if she had quite forgotten where she was or what she should be doing next. Five hours on the go non-stop was beginning to take its toll. The system was demanding a refuel. 'Thanks, Andrew,' she said gratefully. 'I think I must have missed my lunch break, and Sister Guppy isn't on to shoo me off to the canteen.'

In the office she slumped at the desk, trying to summon up the will to seek out Maggie Owen and tell her she was taking half an hour out of the department. The other staff nurse had come on duty at twelve and their hours would overlap for the afternoon.

'Oh, there you are. Haven't you been to lunch yet? Better hurry or there'll be nothing left but bread and scratchit.'

'Maggie! I was just coming to find you.' Helen lifted her head off her arms and beamed at the sight of her friend. 'Got any of that famous bounce and vigour going spare? I'm in dire need of an energy transfusion.'

'Hasn't been *that* bad a morning, has it?' Maggie pulled the duty rota off the wall and took it across to the window. 'We're due for changeover week after next. Not that I much fancy getting up at seven.'

'You'll be glad to swap your late shift for my early shift, though. It can't do much for your social life.'

'My social life—that's a laugh. Bram just asked me if you were going to the Valentine Ball. You! not me. He was telling me what a rave-up it was last year, what a glad time was had by all. D'you know I dreamt about him again last night. We were cleaning up this guy who'd been . . .'

Helen winced and covered her ears. 'Dear Maggie—how you can nurse such passion for that monster beats me. Sorry as I am not to stay and empathise with your nightmares, I feel I must drag along and get a bite and a drink.'

The senior staff nurse was frowning at her reflection in the small mirror behind the filing cabinets, tugging a few more curly strands out of her cap to make a softening frame for her pleasantly plain features. 'Does that look better?' she asked as Helen stood up and crossed to Sister's small hand basin. 'D'you think Bram would go for me a bit more if I lost some of this padding.' She thumped the area around her hips with hopeful fists.

'I wish Bram would go for good!' Helen ran cold water over her wrists and splashed some more over her face. Feeling revitalised she screwed up her paper towel and tossed it with deadly accuracy into the bin. 'Bullseye!'

'Staff nurses at play,' came the laconic drawl from the direction of the doorway. Helen froze. Had he heard that last unguarded remark? The way Bram was jamming up the doorway, it would mean a rather personal squeeze to get past him; something Maggie would enjoy at any rate.

'I'm just going to lunch,' she said shortly, hoping Bram would take the hint and move his bulk.

'I was just saying to Maggie, the Valentine Ball gives

the nursing officers quite a headache, staffing-wise. If you're not going, then I'm sure Miss Raven would be grateful to know if you're available for some extra duty.' A voice hailed him and Bram turned to go.

Maggie giggled and gave Helen an arch look. 'That's not how I read it. He was definitely trying to find out if you'd be there.'

'Probably so he could avoid me like the plague,' said Helen shortly. 'We had something of an exchange first thing this morning.'

'Well, clearly he wants to make amends.' Maggie took over the vacated chair and settled down to check through the report book. '*I* wouldn't mind a row—not if we could kiss and make up later.' She rambled on, oblivious to Helen's discomfiture at a mental image that was a very sore point indeed. 'I can't understand why you two get each other's backs up so. I've never even come close to having a row with Bram. Deep down . . . deep down it could be because you are very attracted to each other. Sort of a love-hate relationship.'

Helen swooped an agitated hand down the neckline of her dress. She pulled out a modest sapphire ring which she wore on a gold chain in working hours. 'I am engaged—remember, Maggie dear?—to Paul Hume. You and your women's magazine psychology! Now I'm off to the canteen. And if there's a major disaster, call me when it's all over!'

Helen was on her way upstairs to say good night to Paul when an urgent pounding at the back door froze her in her tracks. She ran down and got the door open before the desperate caller cracked the panels of frosted glass. Light from the passage illuminated the frightened face of a boy who sang in the choir.

'Tell Father Westcott! He must come quick—our dad's drunk and he's belting our mam somethin' awful!'

The Vicar's study was in darkness.

Vicarage families are accustomed to getting involved in other people's crises. Helen knew her father had calmed the situation before in this particular family; Billy had been right to come here first before dragging in the police. But where was Dad? She peered out across the garden. There had been a light fall of snow. A faint glow illuminated the vestry. 'Let's try in church, Billy.'

They ran together, slipping and sliding on the snowy lawn, pounding through the room where the choir got changed into cassocks and surplices and up the steps to the priests' vestry. Father Westcott was there setting out the vestments for the morning, peering down at Billy over gold-rimmed bifocals and stroking his grizzled beard. He swung his heavy black cloak over his cassock and he and the boy set off, hurrying through the echoing dark aisles. Like Wenceslas and Stephen, thought Helen watching them go.

'Lock up for me, Helen,' called LBW turning back at the doorway. 'The keys are on the vestment chest.' There was a distant crash as the heavy doors fell to behind them and she stood alone for a moment in the nave. Her second brush that day with violent men taking it out on their wives at home. What made men batter? And why did women appear to submit as if there were no alternative? To a modern girl who did not fear to stand up for herself, it was a situation hard to comprehend.

She found the bunch of great iron keys and carefully secured every door of the lofty church. By the time she got up to Paul's flat it was gone midnight.

Paul yawned, his head nodding over the sermon he'd

been working on for Sunday Evensong. 'If this makes *me* go to sleep, heaven help the congregation. Thought you weren't coming to tuck me up tonight. I nearly asked Jenni instead.'

At least he'd boiled the kettle. 'Darling, that really isn't funny. Don't you realise Jenni sees you as Robert Redford and Lawless Lazlo rolled into one?'

There. She had come out with it at last. It was only right he should appreciate the awkwardness of the situation.

Paul looked surprisingly unshocked. He just shook his head, with a rather rueful little smile on his handsome features.

'Lawless Lazlo? Not that hippy chap who's slaying them out in China with his electric harp?'

'Neither Jenni nor I find this situation amusing.' At the sound of her voice, so schoolmarmish and prim, Helen felt ashamed. Paul was too good and kind to be nagged at like this.

Sensing her discomfiture Paul set aside his work and pulled her onto his welcoming lap. He gave her a squeeze and a loving kiss, stroking her cheek with an inky hand. 'Surely you don't suspect me of leading Jenni on?' he questioned in gently chiding tones. 'Clergy learn to cope with female crushes, you know that. It's all part of life's rich pattern. I suppose it's much the same with doctors. We're all caring people and the unhappy gravitate towards us for comfort . . . one just does not take advantage of their vulnerability. Which is not the same thing as avoiding them. Is that what you're asking of me?'

'Jenni is unhappy *because* of you.'

'Jenni is lonely,' came the gentle correction. 'You and Hannah went away—and she sees me as part of the family. Your parents welcomed me into their home, never made me feel excluded. Your father has been like a father to me, your sisters like my sisters. I fear I don't take Jenni's feelings for me very seriously at all. I neither encourage nor discourage.'

'All right. Let's not analyse why this has happened. What can we do to help her through this? It's clearly very painful for her to watch us being happy together. You can't understand the feelings of a teenage girl, Paul. But I can. They run far deeper than you may believe.'

'Would you like some cream crackers and some cheese? You would?' Paul busied himself finding plates and knives and brought them over to the fireside. 'Make you dream,' he teased as Helen tucked in hungrily. 'Now about young Jenni. I think it's time she met a few new faces. There's a lot of uncertainty in her life at the moment—worrying over exams and nursing. And her old boyfriends have gone away to universities and colleges.'

'There's TCYC on Wednesday nights.'

'Far too young and boring to interest Jenni now. What about the medical school? The university isn't far from St Leonard's. You must have medics wandering about on the ward making nuisances of themselves. Don't they have any hops?'

'I don't know much about the university,' said Helen doubtfully. Her face cleared as she thought of something. 'I've had an idea. Why don't we take Jenni along to the Valentine Ball? I take it we are going this year. You know how you love getting a space to yourself and going ape on the dance floor. I might even be able to organise a blind date for her. According to Bram Markland it's a very popular do.'

'Great thinking, doll,' enthused Paul, putting on a

gum-chewing act that had Helen giggling helplessly. 'Free matchmaking service for the bored teenager, courtesy of Helen Westcott, Staff Nurse Extraordinaire . . . Sure I'll take you. Admittedly I hadn't thought that far ahead, what with the Frantics coming up for TCYC's Valentine social.'

'You've got your dinner jacket,' planned Helen. 'And I've got a completely new wardrobe.'

'You've what!'

Helen tickled him under the chin. 'That got you worried. Thought I'd blued my precious savings didn't you, bought myself a whole lot of new clothes.'

Flecks of cream cracker speckled the front of Paul's charcoal grey woollen sweater, and she brushed them away with slim brisk fingers. 'See? When you start a new job, no one knows if your clothes are new or old. So I can wear my Laura Ashley and no one will know it's been to about twenty parties already.'

'You are a tease.' Paul caught hold of her wrist and held it tight in one large strong hand. 'Is that the red Cinderella thing you wore when you passed your SRN exams last year?'

'Charming. You make it sound like something knocked up out of a few rags.'

Paul let go her wrist and went all reminiscent. 'That dress reminds me of the Commem. Balls when I was up at Oxford, punting down the river and dancing the night away.'

'And who did you take in those days before you knew me?'

He went on at such length that finally she could bear it no more and interrupted with a sly, 'Dr Markland was chatting me up today. Asking me about the Valentine Ball. Said I was to save him a dance,' she fibbed, studying her fingernails with one eye on her fiancé's reactions. 'Of course I said I should be delighted.'

It seemed Paul had never heard of an emotion called jealousy. 'Jolly good!' he exclaimed, totally refusing to rise to her bait. 'I'm so pleased you two are getting along better. I knew you must have got it wrong about him disliking you on account of me and LBW being priests. I know Bram's supposed to have a roving eye, and a lifestyle that would make a nun's hair curl—but I've a great respect for the man's professional skills. And I don't set much store by female gossip, at the best of times.

'No,' he continued, resolute in his approval of Bram Markland. 'I've been mighty glad to avail myself of his expertise—and I daresay I shall continue—'

Helen clapped a hand across his mouth. 'Stop it, stop it. This is no frivolous matter. I can't bear to think of you being kicked and trampled and bruised. Or worse. I just cannot bear it.'

Next day when Helen found herself assigned to work with Andrew Lake, she waited for a quiet moment to sound out the possibility of finding a blind date for Jenni. As a senior medical student himself, within a year or so of finishing his clinical studies, who better to know of suitable heartfree young men, pleased to escort a rather shy young girl like Jenni Westcott. Chatting casually Helen discovered Andrew had a younger sister doing her SRN in Cheltenham. She slipped Jenni's name into the conversation and watched for his reaction. But Andrew was turning out to be less shy than he was quiet by nature.

His hand closed over hers and his eyes travelled over her attractive face and figure. 'If it's you wanting an escort, Helen, I'll tell my girl to go home and see her parents for the weekend.

He got his reward. Helen withdrew her hand and aimed a friendly punch at his arm. 'Flatterer!' she said amiably. 'You're too old for my Jenni anyway. She's only seventeen and I was thinking one of the younger students might be interested in a blind date with a very pretty unsophisticated girl. With me hovering around to keep an eye on things.'

'Not with Dr Markland you won't be. I can't see the Lothario of St Leonard's hovering protectively over anybody's kid sister. You want to watch him, Helen, he's dynamite when he gets to work on a girl. And you're far too nice to get strung along with the rest. Now there's a man,' the young dresser couldn't conceal the admiration in his voice, 'who knows how to work hard and play hard . . . Hey, what are you looking at me like that for? What have I said?'

'Andrew Lake!' Helen spelt it out with grim determination. 'Once and for all—I am engaged to one of the hospital chaplains. You may know him—Father Paul Hume. Me going to the Valentine Ball with Bram Markland—the very idea!'

Andrew had the grace to look chastened. He scratched his head and his tone was apologetic. 'That I didn't know. Well, there must be plenty of girls who'd give an eye to be in your shoes. The surgeon *and* the chaplain. Two quite outstanding guys. Of course I've only been working down here the last two weeks. I guess I was mistaken but I kind of sensed an electricity between you and our Dr Markland.' He stumbled on, getting deeper and deeper into a welter of apologies until Helen, desperate to shut him up, suggested it might be as well if Andrew went to the plaster room to give a hand.

'And Andy—do see if you can fix something up for Jenni. No of *course* you haven't been treading where angels fear to. No, my feelings are quite unhurt, you silly. Some kind gentle chap, nobody fast and confident, you understand.'

The dresser looked happier now. 'Leave it with me,' he assured her cheerfully. 'I think I can play Cupid for you. Oh oh. Just listen to that ambulance siren. Sounds like business is on the boom . . .'

What Helen found in the kitchen when she got home on Wednesday was enough to make anyone's hair stand on end.

'Merciful heaven! Whatever have you got there?'

'Fun food for tonight's Frantics,' came the proud explanation from her youngest sister. 'What do you think of those sausages? Paul had the dickens of a job persuading the butcher to dye them green—and those purple porkpies. Don't they look just brilliantly disgusting?'

'I think I may be about to throw up,' said Helen faintly. 'Funny, but before I walked in here I was ravenous. Did Mum make all those red bread rolls? And what's in the fruit pies' pastry? Coffee essence?'

'Nope—gravy browning.' Jenni looked as if she deserved the Chef of the Year award along with three stars from Egon Ronay. 'Hey, someone's banging at the door. Must be the rest of the committee with their goodies for tonight.'

Helen just about managed to stand her ground as saffron meringues and liquorice-black sponge cakes came stomping past her. The blazer-blue doughnuts were the last straw. 'How on earth did you . . . ? No, don't tell me, I'd rather not know.'

'Don't come to the party if you'd rather not,' said Jenni kindly. 'You look awfully whacked to me. But only the committee knows about this, so don't spread the word to anyone else. They're going to be led in in complete darkness. Then when they're tucking in with great mouthfuls of sausage and so on—wham! Paul turns the lights on and everyone—'

'Vomits?' interrupted Helen with succinct brevity. 'What a delightful celebration for St Valentine. Who thought all this up?'

'Father Paul, of course!' came the chorused reply.

'Of *course*, I might have guessed. The last of the great romantics. I think I will have an early night. Jenni can you spare a moment? There's something I'd like to ask you.'

Good as his word, Andrew had organised a date for Jenni. The girl had greeted Helen's suggestion with shrieks of delight, though no mention had been made of a special date arranged for her. Helen decided to wait until she knew if he'd had any success. 'You'll like this one,' he promised. 'Tim Harding—his father holds the Chair of Dentistry at the University. And wait for it, Tim says he knows Jenni already. Met her at a party last winter when he was still at the boys' grammar. He's nineteen and a fresher, living at home.'

'Bless you, you are a darling.' Helen could have kissed Andrew's flushed looking cheek, if he hadn't been so pleased with himself already. Jenni spent most of Saturday getting ready. Helen took things rather more phlegmatically. She decided not to go and watch the afternoon rugby match Paul was captaining, but to slip into the shopping centre for a new lipstick. Something stronger than her favourite bronzy-pink was needed to complement the scarlet of her dress. A silvery eyeshadow would be nice, too, if she could find one at a less than extravagant price. She hurried home, set out her prizes on the dressing table and feeling quite excited at the prospect of the evening ahead washed her hair with shampoo that smelt of lemons. Used her heated roller brush to coax the cornsilk mass into a cascade of deep-curving waves, she was pressing her dress in the kitchen when the telephone rang and Jenni answered.

'I'll just fetch her for you,' she was saying, her voice brightly alert with interest. 'No, she's not at all busy—just doing some ironing. Hold on, Dr Markland.' Then scarcely troubling to cover the mouthpiece and in tones that resounded through the Vicarage, 'Helen! You'll never guess who I've got here. The legend of St Leonard's—and he wants to speak to you-o-o!'

CHAPTER FIVE

HE WANTS me on duty, was Helen's first thought; her second, funny the casualty officer should take the trouble to call her himself. Hey ho, Cinderella won't be going to the Ball tonight after all.

'Hello,' she said with cheerful resignation, never a girl to carp when things weren't going her way. 'What can I do for you, Bram?'

It was the first time they had spoken on the telephone, and she was unprepared for the timbre of his voice. 'Helen?' It came down the line at her, vibrant, husky and enquiring. He sounded incredibly sexy; if you hadn't met the real man you could imagine some charismatic stranger, exciting enough to sweep the most sensible of girls right off her sensible feet. Someone whose concept of pleasure ranged far beyond purple sausages and rugby scrums.

'What will you have first? The good news—' he paused dramatically, 'or the bad.'

Her heart turned a somersault—then began a clog dance against the confines of her ribs. 'Paul!' It came out as a squeak of panic. 'Quickly tell me, Bram. He's really done it this time, hasn't he . . . broken his neck, fractured his skull? Oh, I *knew* something dreadful would happen one day. I told him. I told him—'

Bram held the receiver well away from his ear, pulling a face at the hysterical squawks and splutterings battering his eardrums. So the imperturbable Miss Westcott was not quite so cool after all. She was working herself

THE LEGEND OF DR MARKLAND

up into a considerable passion before he'd even had the chance to . . .

'Shut up, Helen,' he said quite kindly. 'I'm in Sister's office and out there in one of the treatment cubicles is Paul, getting lots of TLC from your good friend Maggie. Bloody but unbowed. I'm looking at the X-ray plates now, they're here in my hand, and Paul's nose is definitely not broken. Or should I say, has not been re-broken. In fact I'm delighted to tell you that noble profile should be as good as ever. Apart from considerable traumatic bleeding—which has ruined the white stripes on his rugger shirt—and two lovely black eyes, there's no real damage.'

Maggie put her head round the office door. 'Tell her I've put it in a bucket of cold water,' she hissed. Bram raised his eyebrows and relayed the message along the line.

'O-o-oh!' wailed Helen, too unhappy to appreciate the wisdom of this. 'My poor darling.'

'There is one problem. He doesn't look too pretty.' Bram paused a moment to let this sink in, then added, 'There's no concussion so I'm not planning on admitting him. I'll get an ambulance to drop him home within the half-hour. Now take a grip on yourself, Helen. Are you ready for the bad news?'

'I hate you, Bram! You're really out to make me suffer.'

'That sounds better, more like the lippy Nurse West-cott I've come to know and love. Well, Helen, your beloved is under doctor's orders. No tripping the light fantastic tonight.' Her indignant splutterings made him smile tolerantly. 'And so, on Paul's *insistence*, I have agreed to provide you with an escort to the Valentine Ball. Myself.'

Helen's face was a picture of disbelief. This had to be some kind of tasteless joke. Her fiancé injured and needing her; and the hospital Casanova planning to step in and do a smooth take-over. 'Over my dead body!' she protested.

'Be ready for eight-thirty, you and your sister. Goodbye.'

There was a distant crash as the hand-set was replaced, a lone buzzing in Helen's incredulous ears. This simply could not be happening. Not to Staff Nurse Westcott, strictly engaged person . . .

But when the ambulance pulled up at the Vicarage gate, and Paul staggered groggily up the path, she saw it was all too true. That beloved face battered and livid, the nostrils packed with gauze. 'Brought you a present, love.' The defiant grin was bashful as a naughty schoolboy's.

Helen held her hand out for the proffered plastic bag containing one sodden and stained rugger shirt. Jenni came running downstairs, took one look and burst into floods of tears. It only served to make Helen crosser. 'He's not badly hurt,' she scolded giving Paul an 'and what did I tell you' glare across her sister's sobbing head. 'Do shut up, you'll mess up your eyes for this evening.'

'But we can't go now,' wailed Jenni. 'Oh Paul—how could you, you've ruined everything.'

'Oh no he hasn't. We're very privileged tonight, Dr Markland's going to escort us instead. Isn't that kind of him?' Helen was still morse-coding rage with her eyes as they settled Paul in comfort with his feet up on the drawing-room sofa. She rushed round lighting the fire, while Jenni fetched a dressing-gown and rugs, and mother made some tea for them all.

'I shall look after Paul tonight,' Mrs Westcott prom-

ised. 'You two go off and enjoy yourselves. You get out
little enough, Helen. And if this very kind person is
going to look after you, then we're all most grateful
to him, aren't we, Paul? What do you feel like eating,
dear? A soft boiled egg with some bread-and-butter
bunnies?'

'Wonderful!' Paul said. 'And Margot, can we watch
the big film together? It's a rare treat for me to see some
television.'

The sisters went up to their bedrooms to get ready for
their treat. Helen slumped gloomily across her duvet
and pondered on a situation that seemed to have got
quite out of control. She'd been going to fling her arms
round Paul, wallow in nursing him, tell him how much
she loved him and how wild horses would not drag her
away with Bram Markland. And what had she done
instead? Make a challenge of the whole thing, as if Paul
had injured himself deliberately so as to ruin their
evening together dancing and socialising with the rest of
the hospital staff. She'd been so looking forward to
showing him off, getting to know new faces, chatting
with people she saw in the corridors and canteen every
day of the week.

And what were they going to think when she walked in
on the arm of Bram Markland, for goodness' sake? That
she was the latest lady in the legendary line of his
amours? Whatever could Paul have been thinking of to
allow this . . . Bram must have made the suggestion in
such a way that Paul couldn't easily have said no.

Yes, that must be it. Having convinced herself of her
fiancé's unwilling part in this charade, Helen decided the
best thing to do would be to get ready quickly, and go
and talk to Paul while mother was busy getting the
supper and he was on his own in the drawing room. She

applied a hasty make-up, grateful for a complexion so fine and flawless that it needed no foundation to enhance its velvet softness; fluffed soft peach blusher over her cheekbones and pewter-glaze shadow over her eyelids, then reached for the new glacé-strawberry lip-polish she had bought that afternoon. A touch of quite unnecessary mascara, perfume dabbed in all the right places (a lovely sultry oriental scent Paul had brought back from a journey abroad) and—apart from zipping up the dress— she'd be ready in a trice.

Helen's bedroom was a chilly cavern large enough to double as a school dormitory. On the deep windowsill stood her old doll's house, on the wall opposite her narrow bed a wardrobe so vast and yawning that her few clothes looked lost by comparison. She lifted down the red dress and stepped into the spreading silky folds, settling the bodice into position. Then struggled with the zip. Breathing hard she took a long critical perusal of her appearance in the full-length wardrobe mirror, not much liking what she saw.

'You look like a strawberry jam tart, Helen Westcott! I didn't know you'd put on so much weight,' she had told her reflection. At the time, the red strapless creation with its tiny waist and heart-shaped bodice had seemed the stuff a girl's dreams were made of. More important the price had been just right. And every time Helen had worn it she had felt good . . . but never had the bodice felt as low-cut and revealing as it seemed tonight. She bit her lip. It would have to do. There simply was no suitable alternative. She wondered what Jenni had come up with. The sewing machine had been whirring into the small hours the last couple of nights.

She slipped on plain silver courts with high thin heels, and sallied down to the amber lamp-lit drawing room to tackle Paul. He was on his own, drowsily watching the news with a pile of old *Punch* magazines at his elbow. 'I want you to know,' she announced, coming into the room and taking up a determined position behind the couch, 'I want you to know, Paul, that I am only doing this for Jenni.'

'Jolly good,' he agreed absent-mindedly, his eyes on the flickering screen.

'It must have been very hard for you, agreeing to let Dr Markland escort me tonight. I want you to know I think you're being very unselfish giving in to him like this. I know,' she added darkly, 'what a bully the man can be.'

Paul gave her a soulful smile and turned back to the TV. 'Just so long as you enjoy yourself, darling.' His head suddenly swung back in her direction. He blinked and stared, blinked again. 'Put all the lights on, will you, Helen? And come round this side so I can admire you . . . my sainted aunt! You look absolutely ravishing. Haven't you put on some weight since last summer? I must say, it does suit you!'

'Oh hell, is it that obvious? I almost couldn't do myself up.' She hitched at the bodice and stared anxiously down at her décolletage. Whatever would Bram make of her? He might think she was *trying* to encourage friendly overtures. Well too bad, she was old enough to look after herself. And who said she must stick with him all evening anyway?

All the same, it was heartbreaking to have to leave Paul behind, looking like a wounded warrior. The bright central light illuminated his bruised and battered eyes and nose, and Helen suddenly noticed a smear of dried blood on his left ear. Her eyes began to moisten and her nose to itch. Hell! this was no time to get weepy, not with the clock standing at eight-twenty and Markland due in ten sickening minutes.

Jenni's grand entrance created a welcome if startling diversion. Paul whistled and Helen said well well, has mother seen it? and Jenni twirled and slunk and was generally delighted by the doubtful look in her older sister's eyes and the knocked-out expression in Paul's. When the doorbell rang the girls were off in a flurry of kisses and have-a-wonderful-times, hurrying out to where Bram had parked outside the vicarage gates.

It was dark and Helen couldn't see him very well, just a tall dark shadowy figure who spoke little and handed them into a rather battered black car that looked nothing very special and typically uncared for. He inquired laconically after Paul, and Helen answered with stiff politeness. Jenni was too excited to speak much as she shivered on the back seat in her mother's fur stole.

'I'll drop you here and find a parking space,' he said when the short drive brought them to the main entrance of St Leonard's. And there by the porter's desk was Andrew Lake with a tall blond youth by his side, pin thin and pleased as punch as his eye fell on Jenni and his hand leapt to fiddle with his black bow tie.

Bram was just coming behind them through the doors. He saw Helen catch her sister by the elbow, whisper something in her ear. And next thing it was as if the world had exploded.

'Blind date? What blind date? Nobody said anything to *me* about a blind date. I'm dancing with Dr Markland when you don't want him.' Jenni wrenched herself away from Helen's grasp and rounded on Bram. 'Isn't that right, Dr Markland? Helen and I are going to share you between us—Paul fixed it, he said so.' She tossed her sunny head, and smiled winningly into the eyes of the man towering over her while turning a determinedly cold bare shoulder in the direction of the transfixed medical students.

Bram struggled desperately to conceal his rising mirth. How old was this pocket Dickensian heroine? Seventeen going on twenty-seven in that awesome little black number. His practised gaze travelled down the skintight black sheath with its one bare shoulder—extraordinary outfit for a childishly slender daughter of the manse. But that hair was a glorious contrast, and the freckled skin translucent against the black satin. And such a ravishing smile, appealing to him to be on her side. He'd better think of something quick before this determined creature stamped her dainty foot right through the polished tiles of Reception.

The porter leaned across the counter and gawped. Helen had gone quite white with mortification, and Tim Harding's skinny neck was red as a cocktail cherry. Bram looked at Andrew and like a double act their hands shot up to conceal their grins.

'Er, you'll have to excuse me, my girlfriend's waiting for me somewhere,' Andrew spluttered and fled for safety.

Jenni turned on the unfortunate Tim and her hazel eyes blazed. 'As for you, Tim Harding, you can take a running jump 'cos I wouldn't dance with you if you were the last boy left on earth. Don't think I've forgotten because I haven't. You heard me, I'm with Dr Markland. Aren't I?'

Bram was thinking he'd never seen such artistic eye make-up other than on a top model. Clever little creature. Taking the child by her sleeved arm he drew her away from the other two, leaving Helen—who was breathing hard enough to split her bodice—fuming with chagrin. This was all in a day's play to Bram Markland. He was loving it with Jenni playing up to him as if the doctor were flavour of the year. She ignored her sister and turned to poor Tim who was fingering his bow tie, rigid with embarrassment.

'Tim, I'm most dreadfully sorry—I've no idea what's got into Jenni. I've never known her be rude like this before, I'm shocked and baffled.' He was such a pleasant-looking young man with his carefully brushed blond hair and smooth fresh complexion, raw bony-looking wrists protruding from the too-short sleeves of his dinner jacket. Clearly the lanky Tim had yet to stop growing. 'Andrew told me you two knew each other, and I—well, I hoped Jenni would be delighted to discover you were her blind date.'

'I'm the one who should be apologising,' he whispered, leaning over to catch the ear of this very pretty older sister. He was sorry she looked so worried and concerned; it was really all his own fault. 'You remember when Jenni used to wear glasses? I'm the one who christened her—' he bit his lip as Helen groaned aloud. The nickname had been all the more hurtful for being so apt . . . Jenni would never forgive Tim for that. There'd been tears about it at home; Mum had written and told Helen the sad tale, wryly bemoaning her youngest daughter's sensitively thin skin. 'Dilly Daydream!' But if she was still a bit of a daydream, Jenni didn't need glasses now.

'It never occurred to me she'd remember. I'd forgotten all about it myself. Even with glasses I thought she was quite adorable—and I leapt at the chance to be her date for tonight . . .' The words trailed away as he saw the look of resignation on Helen's face. The best thing to do, she had decided, was to ask Bram to drive them back home right away. The whole day had been an unmitigated disaster—she just wanted to bury her head in her pillow and let sleep conjure up oblivion.

She stood there miserably, her shoulders slumped beneath her blue donkey jacket (for she'd let Jenni bring mother's moth-eaten fur) her head drooping over the ruination of her scheme. She looked down and found she was holding the stole, her fingers twined helplessly in the soft fur. All this for Jenni's sake—and turning out so dreadfully wrong. Paul would be disappointed, too.

Then Jenni laughed. The sound rang out clear as a bell.

Helen's head shot up. Tim's face turned eager. The sweet nothings Bram had been muttering into Jenni's ear had worked their magic. Her hazel eyes sparkled with delight.

For the first time that evening, Helen looked on Bram with a curious eye. Looked properly. Registered the transformation in his dress. Why, Bram was . . . was sensational. She felt suddenly shy. At least in one area of dress he had some taste, some consideration for the proprieties.

She peeped again, not liking to stare. Anyone could look good, of course, in evening dress *that* expensive. It must have been made to measure in the finest quality materials. The matt-satin lapels, the nipped-in waist emphasising the breadth of his shoulders, the elegant narrowness of the trousers. And that lawn shirt with its snowy ruffle turning the sallow skin to olive. Clearly the sort of clothes, judged Helen, that a Lothario would get most wear out of. Night owl clothes for seductive pursuits . . .

Bram must be well aware how good he looked. Jenni was head-over-heels impressed.

Having poured his oil on Jenni's troubled waters, Bram was even now delivering the girl into Tim's care as though nothing had happened. Helen took her chance and slipped away to the nurses' locker room to get rid of their coats. In the mirror she studied her face and was shocked by her pallor. She hadn't brought any blusher in her evening bag—she'd just have to do.

Let's get this evening over as fast as we can, she mused, hurrying back to the front hall. Everywhere were familiar faces in unfamiliar clothes; you could pass your best friend and not recognise her at a hospital dance. A nurse seemed to take on a whole new identity out of uniform; it was a thought that had often struck Helen in the past. She thought of Maggie, working late tonight on an extra duty to help out. Poor Maggie, how eagerly she would have changed places with Helen tonight, just for the chance to dance in the arms of Dr Markland. Thinking about it sent a cold finger down the channel of her spine. Ordeal rather than pleasure as far as Helen was concerned. Like dancing with a hedgehog, covered with invisible spines.

That little private joke cheered her up somewhat. It was the only way to handle Dr Markland; keep your patience and your sense of humour and you might well survive to tell the tale. Maggie would want to hear all the gory details on Monday.

Bram was lounging by the night porter's booth and Helen was taken aback to perceive the pleasure that illuminated his swarthy features at her approach. Then she remembered he hadn't seen her without her coat and her shoulders hunched with embarrassment over her dress. In fact, it was the first time he, too, had seen her out of uniform—clearly a shock for them both.

Gordon Hanson-White was with him, the hospital's

consultant neurologist, waiting for his wife to emerge from the visitors' powder room. After introductions smoothly presided over by Dr Markland, they moved at Mr Hanson-White's suggestion to the bar, where a noisy crowd had already gathered.

'Were you a nurse?' asked Helen politely of the consultant's surprisingly young and fluffy wife.

'Not me! Haven't a brain in my head, have I, Gordie?' She knocked back a gin-and-french in seconds and had her glass smoothly spirited away by Bram. He winked at Helen as he put the refill into Molly Hanson-White's eager little paw. 'I said, *have* I Gordie? Have I got a brain in my head?'

The eminent neurologist guffawed at the very idea. 'That's why I married you my darling,' he agreed. 'Don't believe in confusing work with pleasure, eh what, Markland.'

Helen felt as if her face was stiff with summoning up polite smiles. Bram must have taken pity on her for he led her off to another group. 'That's Hanson-White's second wife,' he explained. 'He's an ace man, always speaking at international congresses. His children are grown up and his first wife died some years ago. If Molly makes him happy, then good for her. She may be no egg-head but she's mighty decorative.'

'You ought to settle down yourself,' muttered Helen. 'Keep you out of mischief.' She sipped her drink and regarded Bram over the rim of her glass.

His eyes locked with hers. 'Find myself a Molly Hanson-White? You mean a fluffy little blonde?' There was a charged pause while their eyes never wavered. 'I like *my* blondes smooth and cool,' he murmured sensuously. 'And believe me I've already got my eye on a certain one.'

'Ah there you are, Bram. Congratulations on finishing that Paper!' It was the Senior Registrar from Orthopaedics and though Helen saw him almost daily, George Raven clearly hadn't recognised her. She took a step back and tried to look part of the crowd, but Bram wasn't having that.

'You know Helen Westcott, George. Staff Nurse on the A and E Unit.'

George, once he had noticed her, seemed unable to drag his eyes away. 'Helen—of course! Say, what are you doing with this character? Don't you know he's dynamite. Where's our Paul then? Where's that skeleton I've grown to know and love? I've interpreted that many of his wretched X-rays,' he added confidingly, 'I feel I know the man inside out.'

Bram explained her fiancé's absence with such cheerful callousness that Helen could have crowned him with a cricket bat. But she smiled nicely at George and promised him a dance after the supper interval. As yet Bram hadn't shown much inclination to join the dancers, and that was fine by her. He was drinking, true, but not enough to cause concern and for that Helen was more than thankful. If only she could relax; dismiss those feelings of guilt about deserting Paul. It wasn't too difficult to imagine that if circumstances had been different she could have enjoyed the company of the quixotic surgeon.

Watching him with a surreptitious eye as he chatted with his colleagues, Helen wondered how she could ever have found him unappealing. Annoying yes, even infuriating at times—he was all of that. But he had a smile that could melt a girl's heart, if a girl dared let him try. And his looks held a danger all the more potent for the woman who was not free to let herself become involved.

Not for one moment dare Helen relax her guard. She was bound to Paul by the encircling sapphire on the third finger of her left hand. Bram was dangerous because she knew he would try, one day, to break her resolve. He had no compunctions about another man's woman; it would amuse him to test her strength of will. And deep down Helen was frightened.

Professor Rawls was bearing down on them with a purposeful gleam in his eye. 'Was up at last week's meeting of the council of the College of Surgeons,' he boomed. 'Bumped into your old chief. Tells me he hopes to braindrain you from St Leonard's, Markland. Is that true?'

Helen saw her chance and took it, sidling backwards until the throng swallowed her up. Bram wouldn't want her listening in to such a private conversation . . . though it sounded as if he was definitely going. He'd be a fool not to. Imagine Casualty without him! All the drama would go out of life.

Irritated with herself for not being more thrilled to hear the news she would once have prayed for, Helen followed the sounds of music. Bram wouldn't mind if she disappeared. Hundreds of girls must be aching for a dance with him, he'd never even notice she was gone. Kind as it was of Paul, and so typically thoughtful to organise things so she should not be without an escort, it was better to be a wallflower than a clinging ivy.

The strains of music drew her to the canteen. Helen hesitated in the doorway and literally gasped at the sight that met her eyes. Coloured lights were strung across the ceiling making a tent of iridescence. Great swags of artificial mistletoe decorated the walls and swung dizzily overhead attached to shiny red cutout hearts. The whole

atmosphere throbbed with romance and the pounding
sensual rhythm of the dance. Tables had been set around
the perimeter, decked out with candles in bottles,
and red paper cloths—and somewhere in this confusion of heat and bodies and excited laughter must be
Jenni.

A noisy group of revellers surrounded Helen and
swallowed her up before she could explore the length of
the canteen. There were exclamations of surprise that
she was without Paul, but George Raven was there and
he pulled her onto his knee and made the explanations
for her. Helen held her breath, expecting he would tell
the world she'd come with Bram, but it seemed George
had either forgotten or was hoping to make a takeover.
Since Helen felt nothing but easy liking for the ortho-
paedic registrar, she felt happily unthreatened as he
squeezed her waist and nuzzled her bare shoulder. She
could cope with the likes of George.

'There's Jenni!' she exclaimed with relief, pointing
out her sister, who was jiving elegantly in her tight black
dress. Tim looked happy as a sandboy and each was
clearly charmed with the other. The age of miracles,
sighed Helen, thanks to Bram is not quite dead.

'What a little cracker!' applauded George, craning his
neck to watch Jenni's antics. 'I say, isn't that Prof.
Harding's lad she's with?'

Helen nodded and smiled. 'He's a fresher in med.
school. They've known each other for some time . . .
oh!' she gasped as a most ungentle hand descended upon
her bare shoulder, making her wince and recoil. Her
startled eyes travelled up until they reached the level of
the hand's owner . . .

Helen's first thought was that some demonic being
was looming over her and George. Some vampire whose

eyes picked up the coloured lights and flashed red danger signals at her. Defiantly she drained her glass of white wine and chided herself for an over-imaginative fool. It was just Bram in one of his moods. Mouth grim and features scoured with those lines of a tenacious will. 'H-hello Bram!' she shivered, wishing he would take his hand away, waiting for him to spill the beans and tell everyone she was his penance for tonight. But, 'Bram! There you are at last. Sit down with us, Bram. Don't say you're on your own for once,' the chorus welcomed him, and someone scooped one of the nurses onto his lap and offered up the vacated chair.

Helen saw that this was Anne Fallon the black-eyed sister Paul had made much of admiring, pouting now at Bram with her full red lips and tossing her shiny blue-black Cleopatra hairdo. Helen thought she looked far too young and irresponsible to be running Intensive Care, but knew that, on duty, hospital staff assumed an entirely different persona. The Valentine Ball was for letting your hair down and throwing inhibitions to the wind. But though she could feel the silky weight of her own loosened hair on the naked skin of her back, Helen well knew that for this particular staff nurse that was as far as liberation went.

'Where's Deirdre? Haven't you brought Deirdre? Good old Deirdre. C'mon Markland, park yourself right here.'

'Deirdre?' queried someone else, 'she was weeks ago—wasn't she, Bram?'

'Still going round seeing stars though,' giggled the black-eyed Sister Fallon.

Paul wasn't kidding—in uniform or mufti, Anne was blest with stunning good looks. And the way her melting dark eyes slid irresistibly back to linger on Dr Markland told Helen more than a thousand words could convey. All the same she just knew Bram was angry with her. Warily she glanced up.

Smoke erupting from his nostrils and darts of flame from his caustic mouth—nothing would have surprised Helen at that moment. Yes, he was too bound up with his annoyance at being disobeyed, to notice the message Anne was relaying with her bold face and body. But far from breathing fire and brimstone, the doctor looked cool, distant and unamused.

Clearly he would deal with Helen first, let her know he was not a man to be manipulated; then having made his point and avenged his vast ego, he would be ready to honour Anne with his divided attention. A brief shake of his head dismissed the rest of the group.

'I'll join you in a while—but first I'm in need of some exercise.' Helen saw the gleam of satisfaction in his eyes as they captured her unwilling gaze. Now he had got her trapped. 'Let's give George's knees a break, shall we, Helen?'

Anne giggled hysterically at such wit and George complained that Bram was a spoilsport. Helen wondered if her face was as red as her dress and determined Bram's black patent feet should get the benefit of her eight-and-a-half stone at the earliest opportunity. Ungentle fingers had her by the soft flesh above her elbow, steering her towards a space on the dance floor. Pulled her roughly round to face him and grabbed her far too close for comfort.

'Do you mind letting me breathe? My lipstick's going all over your shirt ruffles.'

The doctor relaxed a trifle and Helen drew back as much as he would allow. Her left hand rested on the stuff of his sleeve, her right hand was lost in the cool dryness of his. So many times she had brushed that hand in the impartial exchanges of their work.

'I don't know what you've got to be so cross about—'

'I'm not cross. Have I said I was cross?'

'Not in so many words—but I can tell.'

As he spoke she could feel his warm breath ruffle her hair. He must have smoked a cigar recently, he smelled of good tobacco, masculinity and the lingering traces of Monsieur de Givenchy. 'Since when have you become an expert on my moods?'

'I don't claim any expertise,' countered Helen defensively, 'other than the things one becomes familiar with about a person one works with every day. You're not pleased with me because I'm trying to let you off the hook. You think I wanted to sneak off and leave you, so you're riled. Bram Markland must have the last word and the upper hand. You're the sort of chauvinist who gets your sex a bad name. Now *Paul* had the confidence to—oh! oh my, that was exciting! Can we try that again?'

'Delighted,' muttered Bram, 'if it puts an end to this assassination of my character. Hold on, here we go . . .' With a firm grip on his partner's slender waist he took her into another showy double twirl. 'And now,' he said grimly, 'that you've a captive audience, I'm going to have my pennyworth too. Helen Westcott, I find your suspicion of my motives entirely hurtful. You're a girl who clearly has compassion and sympathy for others, and I like your spirit and your wit. It saves you from being the goody-two shoes I suspected. So give *me* the benefit of the doubt, will you? I'm on my best behaviour tonight. You don't have to run away and hide!'

Helen's resolve softened and her generous heart swelled. She smiled up at Bram and was rewarded with an answering lop-sided grin that for a moment caused her to lose her sense of rhythm and land heavily on Bram's toe, just when hurting the poor man was the last thing she had in mind.

The music changed to a slow-tempo sensuous waltz. Bram drew her very close again, only this time without protest.

To avoid dwelling on what this was doing to her susceptibilities, acutely aware of her body pressed lightly against his, Helen searched restlessly for something to say; anything to keep a dialogue going and destroy a silence that was threatening to become more meaningful with every minute it continued.

'I *wasn't* trying to sneak away,' she insisted, her eyes on a level with the determined set of his elegant shoulders, her sensible nurse's hand lost within his.

'If you say so,' agreed Bram, well-satisfied with himself for having foiled her attempt to give him the slip. Paul probably had not intended that the doctor should be obliged to stick to his fiancée's side throughout the entire evening. And Bram had tactfully pretended a fairly disinterested consent to the request to 'keep an eye on her, there's a good chap. She's only been here a few weeks, and there's young Jenni too.'

He peered down into her cleavage, making not the slightest effort to pretend he was doing anything else.

Helen tried to shrink herself back into her low-cut bodice, mortified at the tell-tale warmth she could feel stealing up her neck. Idiot! she chided herself. You should have tried this dress on before tonight. Half a stone you've got to get rid of, Helen Westcott, before you squeeze into this outfit again. Embarrassed at the way Bram's mahogany gaze was feasting on her face and body, Helen looked anywhere but upward.

'I certainly didn't want to eavesdrop on your private

conversation with Professor Rawls. And I should like you to know I have no intention of cramping your style. Please don't feel you're lumbered with me all evening—there must be quite a harem waiting to dance with you.' Helen listened in shame and horror to the sound of her voice, coming out all piqued and pettish.

'There you go again, Helen,' drawled her partner in that suggestively intimate manner, his mouth burning against her unprotected temple. 'Blackening my character without a shred of evidence. You don't want to believe all you hear about me, you know.'

Helen had the grace to look uncomfortable. 'I don't want to be a millstone round your neck tonight,' she countered stiffly. 'Anne Fallon is clearly dying to attract your attention.'

Bram grinned. 'Really? I hadn't noticed.'

Biting her lower lip, Helen wished she'd had the sense to shut up about Fallon. A dangerously heady excitement was taking over from common sense; Bram's arms were so much more thrilling than George Raven's lap.

'You must have been working extremely hard for your Fellowship exams,' she added hurriedly to take the doctor's mind off Anne Fallon's charms. 'I feel I may have done you an injustice.'

Her ruse worked. 'You were under the impression I was burning the candle at both ends? When the truth of the matter is I've been slaving away into the early hours. I have to admit there've been times I've come into that Unit wondering if I was on my head or my heels,' Bram grimaced ruefully, 'but you did your best to resuscitate me on occasion. Hey!' he chided gently, 'you gone to sleep down there?'

Lifting her head Helen said in a choked voice, 'Sorry, Bram, just my conscience struggling with the odd twinge. Does that mean we shall be losing you as you step on up the ladder to eminence?'

His mouth was just inches from hers as she looked up and he stared down at her, his dark gaze impassive and unreadable. 'Who can say?'

Enigmatic as ever, he was giving nothing away, not to a mere staff nurse at any rate, thought Helen, troubled as never before at the prospect of Casualty without Bram. It would be like food without salt, curry without spice . . .

'Oh look—there's Jenni and Tim. What a relief to see them enjoying themselves,' she said hastily.

'Not as much as I am,' murmured Bram, steering the conversation back onto a light-hearted keel. 'You don't often get the chance of body-contact dancing these days. Those youngsters don't know what they're missing.'

'I don't think they know any of the modern ballroom dances. It does seem a shame,' babbled Helen breathlessly. 'We had classes at the Royal Hanoverian, so if Jenni gets in there she'll be able to pick it up in no time.'

'What a family—yet another daughter ready to pick up the lamp and lay hands on fevered brows. That one,' observed Bram, watching Jenni prancing about with Tim in antics that looked designed to dislocate the spine and cause brain damage, 'looks as if she'll raise some temperatures round the Royal Hanoverian.' He turned his attention back to the girl in his arms. 'Time for some food, don't you think? Not to mention another drink . . .'

CHAPTER SIX

'I DO FEEL a rotten heel,' worried Paul, 'leaving you to
cope with all the services today. And you have two extra
christenings this afternoon as well as Sunday School—
and I can't preach at Evensong as we had planned.' It
was Sunday afternoon and the family was gathered
round the tea table.

'Good gracious, my boy—don't give it another
thought. We just want you better and your old self
again.' The Vicar forced himself to look at his curate's
livid bruises—and shuddered at the far from pretty sight.

Mrs Westcott rested her delicate hand comfortingly
on the young man's brawny wrist. 'It's not your fault,
Paul dear—' She frowned at Helen's disparaging snort of
laughter. 'Well he could hardly kick himself in the face
. . . what was that, Helen?'

'Oh, just muttering to myself, Mother dear. Take no
notice of me.' Helen leaned across and planted a smack-
ing kiss on her fiancé's rather chastened battered cheek.

'The congregation was *so* distressed this morning
when they heard of your injury. "Not again," I heard Mr
Watson remark. No, he didn't say it like that, Helen.
Horrified, he sounded. And some of the old ladies were
distinctly tearful when they saw what had happened to
Paul's handsome face. Of course *we* understand things
look far worse than they actually are—but I did think
you were wise,' Mrs Westcott continued earnestly, be-
stowing on the hapless curate the full force of her
well-meaning attention, 'I did think you were wise to sit

quietly at the back this morning and not take an active part up in the chancel. And Sunday School was quite out of the question—the little ones would have been absolutely terrified at the sight of you. We couldn't risk puddles all over the parquet.'

'Mother, you are a hoot, you really are.' Even LBW was smiling discreetly into his table napkin.

His wife surveyed the table. 'Pass your cup, darling. Give Daddy another scone,' to Jenni, and 'Paul, have some more of Helen's strawberry jam.'

Jenni put in a request for some help that evening with her Biology. 'I've got this genetics problem that's really bugging me.'

The Vicar frowned over his glasses. 'Not another late night please, Jennifer. You've got dark rings round your eyes—get to bed early please, you've school tomorrow.'

His younger daughter looked mutinous. '*He's* got dark circles round his eyes,' she pouted cheekily with a toss of her curly head in Paul's direction. 'But I notice you don't tell him to get to bed early.'

'Enough!' pronounced her father severely, whereupon Jenni fell silent and contented herself with grinning round the table when LBW wasn't looking.

Paul attempted a painful wink at her and stretched out to ruffle the shining head. 'Hear you had a good time last night—and found yourself a most presentable young man into the bargain.'

Jenni turned to him excitedly. 'Yes! And he phoned me this morning. Isn't that amazingly wonderful.' She squeezed her eyes shut and clasped her hands in ecstasy at the memory of it. 'Do you know he thinks I'm stunning without my glasses. Shan't wear *them* again.'

'Except for doing your prep. dear,' interrupted Mrs Westcott with an anxious frown.

Helen and Paul exchanged complicit glances of grati-
fication. As far as the parents were concerned the whole
of Jenni's evening out had been an unqualified success;
and they knew Helen had enjoyed herself too—as far as
was possible without Paul, of course.

Jenni was launching into yet another post mortem,
unable to drag her mind off the Valentine Ball for more
than the odd ten minutes. 'I danced with Bram Markland three times—and he was absolutely divine. In spite
of all the horrible things Helen's said about him *I* think
he's pretty devastating myself. He's very cool, and funny
too—and the way he looks you up and down—oooh, it
just sends shivers through a girl.'

'Yes, well—you've got jam running down your chin.'
An awful dryness had made a sudden desert of Helen's
throat. She passed her cup along for a refill and concentrated on getting the chocolate cake divided into sym-
metrical slices. 'It was quite good fun,' she said in her
brightest tones, 'to see people I work with every day,
dressed up in their finery and relaxing and enjoying
themselves. I hadn't realised how many new friends I've
made over the past few weeks.'

'You'd make friends anywhere, sweetheart.' Paul was
stroking her hand, and his eyes were unusually percep-
tive. He *couldn't* know what had happened. He couldn't
possibly . . . 'You haven't got an enemy in the world.'

Reckon I have now Helen thought. She was silent,
recalling the hatred in Anne Fallon's eyes when Bram
reached past her and held his hand out to Helen for the
last waltz. If Anne wanted to make life extremely difficult for Helen, there was no doubt she'd be delighted to
try . . .

They had danced together in almost complete silence;
and something had crept into her heart with insidious

stealth, releasing her inhibitions and—Helen's generous mouth hardened into lines of shame at the recollection—changing a sensible girl into little better than a hussy. Yet at the time, it had seemed impossible to resist. And mentally wringing one's hands and suffering agonies of conscience wasn't going to alter the fact that she had allowed such a betrayal to go ahead. Had been a willing partner. Was the only one to blame.

They had drifted with the music, away into the darkest corner where she had twined her arms about Bram's neck and there, beneath a dangling sphere of mistletoe, she had let her arch-enemy coax from her a reaction that still shook her to the core. She must have been mad—well, enchanted at the very least. There had never been a kiss like it. And never must be again. Today she felt subdued, chastened, and her feet were very much on the ground. At the first opportunity she must see Bram Markland and apologise for behaving so irresponsibly. Just a kiss. But totally forbidden territory for a girl engaged to be wed.

The duty rotas changed every six weeks, and Monday saw Helen swopping shifts with Maggie and working from twelve noon until eight. This meant coming on when the Casualty day was in full swing, and handing over to the night staff when Sister Guppy was not on a late duty. By five to twelve Helen was in the office, checking the night report and waiting for a quick briefing from Sister who was scribbling furiously at her desk. Maggie had gone to early lunch with two of the student nurses and Bram—well, Helen was puzzled—Bram was nowhere to be seen. Generally he opted for a perfunctory break, well after one p.m. Today he must have changed his mind.

Having geared herself up to speak to the doctor in a quiet moment, thank him politely for squiring her and Jenni, making it clear from her manner that she intended to behave as though that aberration had never taken place—the surgeon's absence came as something of an anticlimax. Like a clock that has been wound up to chime . . . and then misses its moment, thought Helen, feeling the coil of tension within begin to subside. That was the joy of nursing. You could lose yourself in your work; forget about everything else for a solid eight hours—until it hit you as you walked out through the hospital gates.

'It hasn't been written up yet,' said Sister sadly, 'but I know you'll be sorry to hear we've admitted Mrs Harper to Raphael Ward this morning. Fractured femur and pneumonia. I'm afraid I don't give much for her chances. The anaesthetist will have seen her by now, but I'll be very surprised if he considers she can stand an anaesthetic. I've rung your father and warned him.'

Helen's face was pale and shocked. How long had she known Mrs Harper? Fifteen years or more? Staggering up to church as her arthritis got increasingly more painful, yet never a moan or an ill word at her lot. 'What happened? Did she fall on the ice? Oh, and she was being extra careful this winter . . .'

Elsie Guppy shook her head. 'No dear, it didn't happen like that. Apparently she got out of bed in the night to use the commode, fell and couldn't even drag herself to the wall to bang for help. You know what those houses are like in Church Terrace, Victorian built—and built to last. No one heard her calling out.'

'Yes, and the old couple next door are deaf as posts and just as fragile as she is. I don't suppose they're on the phone either. I might pop up to Raphael on my way home.'

'Leave it till tomorrow—there'll be only one visitor she'll want tonight and that's your father. It's kind of you, love, but you ought to get on home while you can, now you're on lates.'

'Poor thing . . . isn't it heartbreaking to think of her lying there all night in the cold, and with her hip broken. And me not two hundred yards away.'

Sister gathered up a pile of forms and tapped them into a neat stack before tethering a rubber band in place. 'Back to what we're here for,' she said briskly, summarising the night report and the morning's activities so her staff nurse was fully in the picture. 'Maggie's gone to early lunch and Dr Markland's taken a few days' leave.'

If her shrewd eyes picked up the tremor that shook Nurse Westcott's dependable frame, they gave no sign. Of course it hadn't escaped Sister Guppy's hearing that since Paul Hume was indisposed Dr Markland had been so kind as to provide a last minute substitute on Saturday night. But deeply fond as she was of all three of these young people, they had their own lives to lead and it was not for her to interfere, whatever her suspicions. She had seen it happen before. You could start off hating someone, as Helen had—for the most unaccountable reasons as far as her colleagues could fathom. A most unusual emotion in a girl whose generous heart and love of her fellow beings was one of her most endearing qualities.

There was such a delicate little line of difference between love and hate, mused Elsie Guppy, from the vantage point of her more mature years. And Helen was still very young, though one tended to forget that because of her poise and her ability . . .

'Dr Gavin Wilson is covering for us,' she told Helen. 'Of course he is not as familiar with the department as Bram; between you and me he's a bit of a worrier, so I'm going to have to shelve some of this paperwork and stick close by. That will mean pushing a bit of extra responsibility on my two staff nurses—but,' and here Elsie demonstrated her confidence in a beaming broad smile, 'that prospect gives me no qualms whatsoever. Have you met Gavin Wilson by the way?'

'No, Sister.'

'He's a very competent general surgeon with a bias towards plastic surgery—ah, Nurse, there you are. Come in, come in! Staff and I are just finishing. Now have you set up those trolleys? You have? Well, I'm going to ask Staff Nurse to check them with you. And then I should like you to clean up that mess in the plaster room. Scrub the floors and wipe down the tables. And don't forget to make sure the trolleys are equipped with bandages ready for the night team before you go off duty at four. Off you go then. Oh, and, Nurse . . .'

'Yes, Sister?'

'Another time you're helping in the plaster room do make sure the floors are well covered with plastic sheets—you will save yourself and others so much time and trouble.'

'Yes, Sister—I'm very sorry, Sister.'

'All right my dear. Just don't let it happen again, will you.'

'N-no, Sister.'

'What was all that about, for goodness' sake?' asked Helen as she shepherded her junior colleague towards the treatment rooms.

Emma Hedge looked astonished. 'You mean Sister didn't tell you? Oh!' she exclaimed fervently, her cheeks turning crimson, 'isn't she a brick. I thought I'd be the laughing stock, but I don't mind you knowing, Staff, so I'll tell *you*.'

Emma, it appeared, had been set to tidy the plaster room and help with any presenting fractures. It had been a lonely and tedious task, for Monday mornings weren't renowned for producing much in the way of bony injuries. And to relieve the monotony the little probationer had decided to plaster her own person. She had only the vaguest idea how one went about the task. The plaster had hardened surprisingly quickly—and Sister Guppy had walked in and found one tearful girl with five white sausages on her left hand and not a clue how to rid herself of them. Not to mention the mess her experiment had created.

'Sister was furious. That awful cold anger. She had to call Dr Robards and *he* thought it was hilarious—you could tell. But when he'd cut the plaster off she made me go and sit in her office and I can tell you, Staff, I felt about so high.' Emma shivered at the memory. 'That's why I've got to set up these trolleys and be tested on them.'

Helen shook her head in amused disbelief. Had her set ever got up to such antics? She supposed they must have in their day, four long years ago. 'What a fun morning you've had, Emma! Never mind, we learn most from our mistakes, so the saying goes. Now this trolley looks fine—the only thing I would suggest is that you add a vomit bowl. Better to be safe than sorry. And you've remembered the Litmus paper. Well done.'

Emma heaved a sigh of relief and they moved on to her next task, a prep tray for a pre-operative shave. Helen was generous with her praise, knowing that positive encouragement was far more effective than negative criticism. She left Emma with her confidence boosted, scrubbing away and crooning the latest number one hit, determined to show everyone she could rise like a phoenix from the ashes of disgrace.

'Go and help Dr Lake with minor injuries and dressings when you've finished. It's my guess you've had enough of the plaster room for one day.' Helen glanced round at all the tools and machinery and, not for the first time, thought it would be no bad plan to try and liven up such a clinical-looking place. No wonder it scared children to be brought in there.

'Dr Lake? Oh, you mean Andrew, the dresser. Yes, okay, Staff, will do. Sounds funny though when people say *Doctor* Lake, I always think. He's not a trained doctor yet.'

'And you're not a trained nurse yet, Nurse Hedge. But it gives patients greater confidence in Andrew if we allow him the courtesy title. Now I'm going to let Sister know you've done well, so don't let us down, there's a dear.'

By five o'clock Helen was feeling decidedly peckish. As she went off for her tea break, passing the pigeon holes where the post was sorted, she stopped to see if there might be an airmail from her best friend Sue Kyme. She had flown out to the States to take up a job in a burns unit in Texas, and Helen who had heard nothing from her at Christmas was feeling concerned at Sue's silence. Not knowing whether Sue would write to the hospital or her home address Helen was being careful to keep a check on the pigeon holes. There was no airmail; but there was one white handwritten envelope, with her name, Miss Helen Westcott, in a black scrawl Helen just knew she'd seen somewhere before . . .

It could wait till she got off duty. She stuffed it into her

pocket as another nurse hailed her, and they hurried
along to the canteen together.

'Saw you with Bram Markland on Saturday night,'
said the nosy staff nurse on Gynae. who liked nothing
better than to nourish the grapevine with gossip.

Not knowing her all that well, Helen was not aware of
this. All the same she chose her words carefully and was
studiedly non-committal. 'It was a last minute arrange-
ment when my fiancé got injured in a rugger match. I
think he rather twisted poor Dr Markland's arm getting
him to escort me and my young sister . . . I wasn't at all
bothered about missing out, but we didn't want Jenni to
be disappointed.'

'She is lovely, isn't she—not a bit like you to look at.'

If the other nurse had expected Helen to look put out
at that ambiguously phrased comment, she was in for a
disappointment for Helen just grinned and chuckled her
agreement. At the same time she was becoming aware
the conversation concealed undertones to be wary of—
and next moment this suspicion was confirmed.

'Anne Fallon is a good friend of mine,' she remarked,
pushing open the door for Helen and letting her go in
first. 'You know Anne of course—she told me you were
with her group on Saturday night. Enjoying yourself I
hear by all accounts. Making up to Bram Markland.'

They were queuing at the serving counter, trays at the
ready. Helen stared with queasy dislike at the containers
offering greasy chips, greying tinned peas reheated from
lunch-time; sticky charred sausages and dry-looking
pork chops. What ever was the matter these days with an
appetite that could have managed a horse not so long
ago?

If she could have walked out there and then and
escaped from her tormentor she would have gladly done

so. But here she was, trapped in a hungry line of late-shifters eager to sink their teeth into an early supper. With this woman watching her with sly probing eyes.

'Your friend has a vivid imagination.' Helen managed to keep up a calmly unperturbed countenance; but her heart was pumping fit to bust. She reached the till with one pot of honey yoghurt, an apple, roll and butter. Paid for her snack and headed deliberately across to a table with just one empty chair, avoiding with bent head the triumphant expression on the staff nurse's face as she sauntered past with her own loaded tray.

It was almost half an hour late when Helen finally got off duty. As the senior nurse she was responsible for leaving the department shipshape for the oncoming nursing team, and for delivering the report that prepared them for taking over from the day staff. She had stayed to give an extra pair of hands with a gastric lavage performed on a would-be suicide; an unpleasant procedure that must be made as untraumatic as possible for the desperate patient. It was depressing but life-saving work, and that final physical effort drained Helen of her diminished vitality.

She took the lift up to the third floor and was just stepping out into the corridor, deserted except for the last straggle of visitors, when her father, wrapped in his voluminous black cloak and with his head bowed over something he carried muffled in the folds of his cloak, came towards her from the direction of the stairs. Without any sign of recognition he passed and Helen with a sinking heart saw him turn into the entrance of Raphael Ward. She knew he must speak to no one and that he brought the last sacraments to Mrs Harper . . . well, there was no purpose in her speaking to the night staff now. Sister Guppy had not been wrong in her prognosis.

Helen got a shock as she wheeled her cycle through the hospital gates. A parked car flashed its lights at her and for one trembling moment she thought . . .

Then she recognised Paul's curly head in silhouette against the lamplight, at the wheel of her father's ancient Morris. He wound down the window and hailed her as she crossed over to speak to him. Helen peered at him anxiously in the dark, but his bruises were indiscernible in the shadowy interior. 'How *are* you, Paul darling? I can't see you properly in there.'

'I'm absolutely fine—just so long as I don't catch your father's cold and have to blow my nose! Now why not park your bike and have a lift home. I can come back for LBW later. He's with Mrs Harper . . . I expect Sister Guppy—'

'Yes, Paul, she told me. I went up to Raphael and saw him going in, so I came away. Look, I won't waste Dad's precious petrol, I'll get on home. I could do with a long soak in the bath and an early night.'

'Right you are, sweetheart. I won't disturb you when I come in. Now give us a kiss before you go . . .'

Helen obliged. 'Wind that window up before you catch your death. 'Night, Paul.'

He called her back as she turned to go. 'Almost forgot. Your supper's in the oven and your mother says if you want pudding you'll find some cold rice and stewed pears in the pantry. She's playing the piano for a sing-song, round at Willowfarm, for the old folk . . . and by the way, Jenni has a visitor.'

'Not—?'

'None other. Didn't you do well!'

'Didn't Andrew Lake do well, bless his cotton socks.'

She should never have mentioned socks. All the way home Helen's imagination was full of Bram and his multi-coloured feet. She'd never thought to check his socks on Saturday—but presumably he found it easy enough to match black with black! Where she had once been so disapproving of his scruffy attire, it now struck her as engagingly idiosyncratic. He was one of nature's individuals—and so was Paul. It took all sorts to make a world—and the world was the better place for having people with such dissimilar but powerful personalities . . .

Where had Bram gone? Why had he not mentioned the fact that he intended to take some leave owing to him? How long would he be away? Sister had simply said 'a few days' . . .

Back home Helen hung up her jacket and discovered that letter along with her purse in her pocket. A thread of light beneath the drawing room door showed Jenni was entertaining Tim in style. Helen didn't want to pry, but she supposed she should say hello and offer the two some coffee. But first . . .

She went wearily up to her room, searched out that plastic tube of Vitamin C, and climbed on up to Paul's darkened attic flat.

Leaving the tablets prominently where he couldn't fail to find them—on his pillow—she glanced round the monkish bedroom with its bare floorboards, crucifix over the iron bedstead, and brown cotton coverlet. A cold was the last thing he needed with that damaged nose; and Dad must take some Vitamin C too, to get rid of his cold before it settled in the usual place: on his bronchitic chest—the smokers' weakness.

Tim and Jenni were playing Scrabble, more politely formal than they had been on the dance floor. If she had suggested champagne cocktails for two they couldn't have responded to her suggestion with greater alacrity. Helen found herself remembering nostalgically those times when she too hadn't been able to eat or sleep, in the throes of first love. It hadn't been like that with Paul. He'd been part of the family long before they decided to marry; and that decision hadn't had any ill-effect on her very healthy appetite . . .

It was Bram who was sending up her emotional temperature these days in a manner she'd never have believed possible, mused Helen ruefully, peering disinterestedly at a deliciously creamy rice pudding. She just wasn't her old calm self any more. She made the children's coffee, picked at her liver and bacon, and dragged her weary limbs up to the bathroom, yearning for a long—and preferably dreamless—sleep.

'Did I leave a letter on the table, Mother dear? White envelope with black-inked writing . . .' Helen was prowling round searching for the letter she so carelessly kept forgetting to read, cup of coffee in one hand as she moved the butter dish and peered behind the salt-and-pepper pots.

Margot Westcott drummed her fingers on the table as she surveyed the scene with a considering air. 'There was a letter . . . but you know what I am. Whatever would I have done with it now?' Her face brightened. 'I remember—I put it underneath your ironing where you'd be sure to find it. Look! here we are.' She swept aside a pile of shirts and blouses which Helen was going to tackle after breakfast. 'Can't think why people accuse me of being vague and forgetful, it's most unjust.'

Her daughter looked up from studying the by now rather crumpled envelope. For some strange reason she thought she'd better open it where she was alone. 'Mother dear,' she commiserated, 'you have a perfectly good memory. It's just you have too much to do. And that,' she pointed out sternly, 'is because you say yes to everything anyone asks. If you were a businessman you'd have a secretary to point you in the right direction and organise your diary. Look at all the times you double-book yourself for this, that and the other. Honestly, who'd want to be a vicar's wife in a busy city parish.'

'Good heavens dear, that's an odd remark to come from you!' Mrs Westcott was tying a scarf over her hair and exchanging her eternal sandals for a pair of elderly suede boots. She had a penchant for woollen tights to match her artistic inclinations, and today her thin legs were sheathed in henna-colour tights. She was off to help clean the church with the other ladies of the cleaning roster.

'When I've finished the ironing I'll see to Paul's flat,' Helen decided aloud when her mother had gone. 'Lord, she's forgotten her dusters.' Picking up the cloths she rushed after Mrs Westcott, and again the letter got forgotten as the ironing absorbed her attention. And it was only when the last shirt was hanging neatly ready to be taken up to Paul's flat, that she got round to slitting the envelope and pulling out a single folded sheet of expensive watermarked notepaper. Her eyes glanced over the assertively masculine hand and skipped on down to the signature. Bram Markland . . . Bram! Why ever would Bram be . . . but even before she had read one word Helen's hands were shaking and a pulsebeat fluttered in her throat.

Helen—I think we both agree we have to talk. I shall be on interview in London when you read this. Stay behind

on Saturday when you finish your late duty. Yours,
Bram.

'Yours, Bram. Yours . . .' she repeated—terrified at
the implication. He was wrong—they had nothing to talk
about, nothing to admit to each other. Helen grabbed a
piece of kitchen roll and gave her nose a punishing blow,
her eyes full of tears and her heart aching with a heavy
dull pain. So Bram was being interviewed by his old
hospital after all: that must mean he would definitely
leave St Leonard's. She supposed they would ask for
three months notice—that was the usual time for senior
medical staff.

Feverishly she calculated when he would go. End of
May at the latest. Then she would be free—and her
turbulent emotions would once more return to an even
keel. It was just an overwhelming physical attraction.
She loved Paul Hume. She was 'in love' with Bram—yes,
there was no denying it. There was a physical chemistry
between them that was all but irresistible, and each
knew the other was aware of their feelings.

Helen had cleared the breakfast table and begun to
wash the dishes without being aware of what she was
doing; moving like an automaton programmed to wash
and rinse and wipe . . . *Saturday*, she breathed, unable
to check her foolish imaginings . . . *Saturday*. At least
she knew she would see Bram then: and make it
clear there would never be anything serious between
them.

By the time Paul's shirts had been neatly put away in
his wardrobe and the vacuum cleaner was roaring
furiously round his rooms, Helen had worked herself
into a state of indignation. So Bram had the confounded
cheek to believe she would drop everything just for the
honour of being selected 'girl of the moment'! The

insufferable arrogance of the man. Who did he think he was?

And if the truth were known Helen was blaming herself even more. What a little idiot to let his practised seduction techniques go so swiftly to her head. It wasn't even as if she had the excuse of being a young probationer: new to nursing, and new to working with these glamorous beings called doctors. (It didn't take more than a few weeks for *that* particular myth to bite the dust.)

As for the legend of Bram Markland . . . You should have grown out of fairy tales at your age, Helen scolded herself with merciless derision and a curl of prettily pouting lip. Since the wretched man's soon to be gone, the hospital grapevine will have to find some new idol to fantasise about and feed on. She squirted furniture polish over Paul's desk and in a fury of energy and elbow grease rubbed and dusted and polished till the whole flat shone clean and bright as the proverbial new pin. And her whirlwind of activity satisfactorily completed, Helen shut the door on her efforts and hurried to her own room to get ready for work.

She might have felt less resolute and clear-headed, had she noticed what had fallen from her pocket onto Paul's bathroom floor . . .

CHAPTER SEVEN

PAUL HAD waited for more than an hour that morning in Casualty to have the check-up Bram had requested. His appointment card said nine; but although the department didn't seem especially pressured he wasn't called until well after ten. Not one of the junior nurses, drifting about with navy cardigans slung across their shoulders, recognised him sitting there at the back, casually dressed in jeans and a dark Guernsey sweater. Paul felt a bit like the invisible man, without his cassock and dog collar. A couple of times Staff Nurse Owen whisked through the department—but he didn't like to accost her even to say hello, in case others suspected him of trying to jump the queue. Sister Guppy must be at her Monday morning meeting with the Senior Nursing Officers.

In the event he had to sit out the irksome wait, itching though he was to get on with things after that enforced weekend of idleness. He didn't even get to see Dr Markland in person. Not that it really mattered since he was clearly on the mend.

He cycled home, racing downhill into the wind, only his narrowed eyes visible under the grey balaclava Mrs Westcott had knitted him for Christmas. Propped the sports bike by the back door—and with athletic strides of his long powerful legs bounded the two flights of stairs to grab some quick elevenses before starting his list of visits.

No one was about—though splashing noises had come from the direction of the bathroom as he crossed the landing on the first floor. Paul flung wide his bedroom door and sniffed appreciatively at the smell of beeswax hanging on the air. His books and papers were arranged tidily—not a trace of dust or fluff on shelves or floor; and every polished surface was glowing from a mixture of elbowgrease and beeswax. Helen was an angel, no doubt about it. Not many girls would do this for a man before tackling an arduous day's nursing.

Paul dragged off the balaclava, his curls springing up like crushed and rumpled feathers. Strode to the bathroom, kettle in hand. Stooped to pick up the one untidy object in the entire flat—a folded white envelope with Helen's name written on the front. Filled the kettle with just enough water for one person; plugged it into the socket and smoothed the creased envelope before sticking it on the shelf behind his grandfather's pewter tankard. Next he spooned a careless mix of coffee and sugar into a mug—and five minutes later was back on his bike and heading out into the wind.

It was only when she was pinning up her freshly-washed hair into the usual on-duty french pleat that Helen remembered she hadn't actually *got* the letter that had been dwelling on her mind for the past couple of hours. And it was after a fruitless search through all her pockets and the rooms she'd been into that morning, that the awful thought occurred to her that she could possibly have dropped Bram's letter up in Paul's flat. She'd heard him race in and out again before she'd had the chance to ask how he'd got on up at the hospital, being busily drying her mane of hair at the time.

Paul never locked his rooms. He insisted he'd got nothing any burglar would give a thank you for. And anyway none of the family would dream of prying. For once Helen felt like a sneak thief, leaning back against the closed door, her eyes darting everywhere like a cornered animal, not knowing where to start looking for that treacherous telltale envelope . . .

But the envelope was almost the first thing she saw, propped there on the shelf where Paul had discovered it in haste and left it to pass on to Helen later. But . . . had he read it? Knowing well the sort of person he was, Helen guessed Paul was in too much of a hurry to give the matter a second's thought: and he would never dream of reading private correspondence, whatever the circumstances. Supposing though he assumed it was his own—and why not? in the confines of his own room, not seeing the inscription on the front and without much thought on the matter, supposing he had glanced briefly at its contents to remind himself who had written, and why. Only then to discover his mistake, when confronted with that tersely personal message to his fiancée.

Sick and wretched with her own carelessness Helen knew this was a problem one could mull over for hours: and all she'd got was thirty minutes before she must report for duty.

To snatch the letter back would be to rouse Paul's interest. He would realise it was of some particular significance, and in all innocence be bound to ask why. Just a polite enquiry of a girl to whom he was supposed to be closer than to anyone else in the world. And of course it would be easy enough to invent some story to satisfy an idle query . . . But did she want to involve them both in a tissue of lies that could only increase her own feelings of disgust and self-reproach?

No, she was quite certain she did not.

It took a good deal of courage as with a heavy sigh Helen closed the door, leaving that envelope where she had discovered it. Knowing it would be some twelve hours before she could know whether Paul would—or already had—read those incriminating lines.

If, she resolved—if he had, then she must confess to him, absolve herself, seek his forgiveness. Open her heart and admit all the secrets it held close. Tell him, *reassure* him she would never let Bram mean anything to her again—even if it meant giving in her resignation. At all costs Paul must not be hurt by any of this. Together it would prove a minor squall in the tempests of life—and they could weather the storm.

Sister Guppy was working split shifts, which meant she would resume duty at four when Maggie went off, giving the department two senior nurses all day. For the first time in her life, Helen was ten minutes late reporting for duty.

And almost too worried to care. She hung her cloak in the staff changing room and went to seek out Maggie Owen who was not to be found in the office. Between them they decided how to organise the afternoon. Maggie as Senior, should co-ordinate the nursing staff and keep herself free to patrol, as Sister did; overseeing the diversity of skills so that all personnel worked efficiently together, and keeping open the lines of communication that linked the A & E Unit with the rest of St Leonard's Hospital.

'If you, Helen, work with Dr Robards I can then put a senior student to help Gavin Wilson. That way we have a senior doctor with a less experienced nurse, and vice versa.'

Helen was quite conversant with correct procedure; which stipulated a blend of relative degrees of experience, so that a staff nurse was best deployed in assisting a junior casualty officer while a senior student nurse would be set to work with the duty officer in charge. All the same . . .

'You don't think that as Dr Wilson is so jumpy without Sister here, that it might be as well for me to take the brunt rather than let a student.' She grimaced, not relishing the job, but prepared to do whatever seemed best—given the circumstances and the staffing available.

She put her hands together in an attitude of mock-prayer and raised her eyes to the ceiling. 'Come back, Bram—all is forgiven!'

Maggie laughed and swallowed a quick glass of water straight from the tap—the only drink she'd had time for since mid-morning break. 'No need to sacrifice yourself, duckie—I'll keep an eye on Gavin. Can't wrap these third-year nurses in cotton wool, can we? If they can't stand the heat they should keep out of the kitchen.'

But an hour later Maggie's cheerful confidence was being sorely tested. Helen took one look at the red spots high on the staff nurse's cheeks and teased, 'What's up with you then? Don't you like playing acting Sister after all?'

'I appreciate that the guy isn't used to us,' exploded Maggie in a head of steam. 'But does he have to behave like a neurotic giraffe just because Sister's having an afternoon off?'

Helen chuckled sympathetically. She took an empty bottle from the medicine cupboard, sniffed the dregs, pulled a sour face and rinsed it under a running tap. 'What's Dr Wilson done now?'

'It's not what he does it's what he says.' Maggie pulled out a hankie and wiped her sweating forehead. 'Every five minutes he's got to check on this and that. If he asks me just once more if I've sent his precious blood gas to the lab, so help me—I'll . . . I'll swing for him. I mean is it *my* fault the A & E Unit at the General has its own blood gas analyser? You'd think I was responsible for the inadequacies of our equipment the way he carries on.'

Dumping the empties into the dispensary basket Helen closed and locked the drugs cupboard and gave Maggie the keys. 'I bet you haven't had any lunch, have you?' she said sympathetically. 'Never mind, you're off in an hour. Better go and grab a bite then. D'you think we've time for a quick coffee? Oh—oh, definitely not!' she exclaimed, as the sound of an ambulance siren rapidly approaching broke into their few stolen moments of tranquillity.

'I'll see to this one,' said Maggie, her old brisk self again. 'You keep the non-emergencies moving along.'

'Right you are,' said Helen and went off to check the state of reception.

Procedure was for patients not presenting as immediate emergencies and travelling to Casualty under their own steam, to register at the reception desk manned by two clerks. Stretcher cases, or those patients brought in by ambulance, were wheeled in via a separate entrance that admitted them directly into the emergency area. A student nurse would come to the door and call by name for patients waiting in the rows of chairs for their turn to be seen for treatment. Helen spent the rest of the afternoon supervising this area until Sister Guppy arrived to complete her split shift, bringing gladness to the heart of the acting senior casualty officer and blessed relief to Maggie Owen.

By now Helen was getting accustomed to supper in the kitchen alone—though the vicarage was not exactly empty. There was Jenni and her girlfriends gossiping up in the bedrooms, doing each others' hair and playing records; the Vicar closeted in the study interviewing couples wanting to get wed in Holy Trinity at Easter; and Mother with the rest of the Working Party committee earnestly discussing the next Sale of Work round the dining room table. Paul, with the help of a small electric fire, was over in the vestry taking a confirmation class through the teachings of the Catechism while an inquisitive mouse tried with some success to sabotage proceedings—until Paul got cross with the girls and threatened to dampen their hysteria with a jug of icy water.

Left to her own devices, Helen washed up the supper things and turned on the television to watch a documentary about the problems of the health service. Then, as Paul was still not home, having gone for a quick pint with some of the older members of his class, she settled down with a couple of nursing journals to catch up with the latest news in nursing processes. They proved interesting enough to take her mind off the one problem bothering her most: the immediate dilemma of the letter upstairs in Paul's flat.

She need hardly have worried, Helen told herself later, with an ironic sense of the way fate could sometimes be thwarted in its intent. For, when she joined her fiancé for their customary quiet half-hour together at the end of the day, that white envelope was exactly where it had been left . . . all the same it was the first thing Helen's anxious gaze fastened upon when she walked into the flat. If her voice sounded artificial, only she noticed, trying to seem pleased—but not *too* pleased— to discover it there on Paul's shelf. 'I was wondering where that had got to. Must have dropped it when I was cleaning.'

'You made a wonderful job of the flat, darling,' said Paul gratefully through a mouthful of crumbs. 'Quite a transformation of my usual squalor.' This was a gross exaggeration, for he was a man of few possessions—having things was of little importance to his rather ascetic tastes—and by nature he preferred to live tidily. 'I found that envelope on the bathroom floor. See, it's got your name on the front.'

'I know.' Helen tucked the wretched thing deep into her skirt pocket, miserable at Paul's innocent lack of suspicion. Hating herself for the wrong she was doing to such a good and simple person, and hating Bram Markland for being a complicated no-good fascinating bastard. It occurred to Helen that even if Paul *had* read her private correspondence—which so manifestly he had not—in his innocence he would doubtless see nothing untoward in Dr Markland seeking mysterious assignations with his own beloved.

'Here you are, my pet.' Paul thrust into Helen's quaking hands a plate of cheese and digestive biscuits. 'I'll just wash these apples.' Humming a plainsong chant he disappeared into the bathroom and Helen could hear the sound of the taps running and water being splashed liberally over her freshly polished lino. Not knowing whether to laugh or cry, she picked laughter as the preferable alternative and snuggled up to Paul when he joined her on the couch.

'I take it Dr Wilson gave you the all-clear this morning?' She touched with delicate fingers the yellowing bruises that were fading fast. 'Does that hurt at all?'

Paul shook his head. 'Dr Wilson? so that's who it was. I wondered where old Bram had got to.'

'I think he may be in London being interviewed for a post at his old teaching hospital. Here—let me do that for you.' She peeled the apples and quartered them precisely, her lowered eyelashes shielding her thoughts from Paul's sudden alert gaze.

'Over an hour I sat there twiddling my thumbs,' he was recalling ruefully, apparently grieving more over his wasted time than the prospect of Markland moving on and up in his hospital career. 'I sometimes wonder why you people bother to give out appointments when you've no inclination to stick by them. The place was quiet enough. Scarcely saw another patient—let alone a nurse!'

Helen sighed and explained and defended the system. 'Sitting out there, you don't know what we're coping with behind the scenes in the treatment rooms or in the emergency area. For all you know, there could have been a major disaster with all hands on deck. You wouldn't necessarily see anything, because the ambulances bring people in by stretcher via the emergency entrance.' She patted his hand in an admonishing fashion. 'Come on, darling! You've been brought in wounded yourself enough times to know very well there's more to our unit than just rows of chairs and the reception desk. Now if only we had more staff—'

'I know, I know,' mumbled Paul through a mouthful of cheddar. 'If you had more staff . . . the old story. I suppose I'd hoped for a bit of VIP treatment seeing I'm a familiar face around St Leonard's in my professional capacity. Maggie and Elsie generally make rather a fuss of me when I'm brought in feet first, but they were nowhere to be seen. And,' he added in hurt fashion, 'no one seemed to recognise me in mufti!'

Helen giggled. 'Denims do have rather a different image from a cassock. And I don't like to hear you talking as if you're a regular customer, Paul Hume.

Promise me you're going to keep out of trouble for the rest of the season.'

'I promise—cub's honour!'

Helen's next day in the Unit went much as any other. Periods of hectic activity with everyone working at full stretch, their professional skills and stamina tested to the limit; interspersed with a few low pressure troughs allowing everyone to get a second wind and tidy and restock the department. During one of these oases of quiet when Helen was putting cubicles straight and checking up on the treatment rooms, she found herself thinking of Bram. He would be back on Saturday—and expecting her to meet him when she came off duty. Her breath quickened as her mind's eye replayed the image of that terse letter: 'we both agree we have to talk'.

We *both* agree we have to talk.

She came to a sudden decision. What was there to talk about? No, she didn't agree with Bram Markland—not on almost any subject you cared to name. It was so simple really. No compulsion either. All she had to do was slip away punctually, without bothering to change her uniform. Get to the cycle shed and be home before Bram even realised she wasn't going to turn up after all . . .

Having made her decision Helen felt much better. It didn't solve the problem of her inner turmoil, her pent-up longing to be in his arms again. But at least it was a safe option, the coward's way out.

'I'm off now,' declared Maggie at two minutes to four, glancing up at the clock which was running a little slow. She peered out of the window and swore colourfully. 'That's right, blizzard, wait for Maggie Owen to come out and play . . . Now I suppose all the buses'll be up the creek.'

'You're in a rush tonight. Going somewhere special?'

'There's a sale on, starting today, at that flash Italian shoe shop in Buttle Street. I wanted something snazzy for my brother's wedding next month. Now look at it, I shall never get there before closing time if this lot keeps up.'

Helen peered out of the window into a swirling mass of snowflakes, and grimaced at the thought of the home-bound traffic that would soon be getting under way. All that snow falling on already icy roads . . . 'We're going to be in for a busy night. I'd better go and put out more sets of equipment and get the girls to lay up extra trolleys.'

'If you need me—send me a postcard! 'Bye Helen, I'll see you tomorrow.'

As it happened Maggie was wrong. She was going to see Helen again very shortly—and in circumstances that would take both nurses completely by surprise.

CHAPTER EIGHT

HELEN tore the wrapping off the rolled-up bandage.

'If you come back to Casualty in a couple of days, we'll have a look at the dressing and make any necessary adjustments. In the meantime you should rest that leg as much as you can.'

The young mother grimaced and tucked a loose strand of hair behind her ear. 'That's a laugh, that is, Nurse. I've got three little ones under five, and my Steve's a long-haul lorry driver. Never mind,' she added, seeing the concern that flooded the nurse's gentle face, 'you got enough to do without worrying about my problems. My Nan lives a few streets away, she'll lend a hand.'

'You sure?' Helen strapped the bandage into place with a length of surgical tape. 'I could ask the social worker to have a word with you.'

'No, love, no. It'll be okay.' She made as if to climb down from the treatment couch—but Helen stayed her with an outstretched hand. She went to the lock-up cabinet outside the cubicle and came back with a pre-packed syringe of tetanus vaccine.

'Dr Robards ordered a tetanus jab—if you haven't had one recently.'

The woman frowned, trying to remember. Just a few years older than me, thought Helen, and already with three babies to cope with. How on earth is she going to manage, with that leg?

'I can't recall when I last . . . well, I think it must have been when I was about twelve and stood on a rusty nail in the garden.'

'In that case,' said Helen, taking the cover off the needle, 'this won't take a moment. Better to be safe than sorry. There's a risk you could get lockjaw.' One sure movement and the injection was given and the patient was on her feet again, testing her weight on the deeply gashed leg.

Before going for her tea-break Helen looked into the Emergency Room, and seeing that it was empty switched on all the lights for a swift check round. Six beds stood ranged along one wall ready to be used in the event of a major crisis—with extra bed rolls stacked on tables in case they were needed. The junior nurses had aligned trolleys and wheelchairs neatly, as Sister Guppy decreed, and the metal cupboards were stocked with their full complement of drugs and dressing packs and emergency surgical equipment. All was meticulous, all was serene; yet Helen knew only too well how that calm would be shattered as the department swung into organised action in the event of a harrowing motorway smash, or some similar disaster involving multiple casualties.

Satisfied that the Unit was as ever prepared and ready to cope, she doused the lights and stepped out into the harsh fluorescence of the corridor . . .

And there towards her came an apparition that could not have been more shocking had it been a spectre with its head tucked underneath its arm!

Bram, grim as death, with the limp body of Staff Nurse Owen dangling heavily in his arms . . .

'Get that door open quickly! She weighs a ton.'

Helen moved like an automat trained to face emergencies. But her mind was one shriek of alarm.

'I ran her over.'

Bram staggered across to the nearest bed and lowered the unconscious staff nurse carefully onto the red blanket. He unfastened Maggie's thick tweed coat and made a thorough examination of her head, her limbs and her insensible body.

'You ran her over?' Appalled by that bluntly expressed admission, Helen's imagination ran riot. The cold-blooded criminal, the heartless beast . . . what was he doing there anyway? Bram Markland was supposed to be in London.

Her frightened gaze raked the doctor's sombre face as he bent over Maggie. Maggie groaned, opened her eyes and tried to sit up. Amazement dawned as she looked first at Bram, then at Helen's expressive face flushed with shock and anger—then at the awesome familiarity of the Emergency Room.

'Bloody hell!' she said with her usual earthy matter-of-fact tones. 'What on earth have you brought me in here for?' Before either of the onlookers could stop her, Maggie swung her legs over the edge of the bed, tried to stand up—and slithered to the floor in a most ungraceful heap as her left ankle refused to take her weight. Whereupon she immediately fainted a second time.

'Now I've got to pick her up again!' exclaimed Bram. 'Who does Maggie think I am, King of the Amazons?'

Instantly Helen was on her knees, lifting Maggie's head and glaring reproachfully up at Bram. 'If you ask me she's broken that ankle—and all you can do is make wisecracks because you're too feeble to pick her up.' Together they heaved Maggie back onto the bed and with cautious fingers Helen began working on the zip of the left suede boot.

'Have a heart, I carried her all the way here from the front gate.'

'You knocked her down!'

'I didn't. I said I ran over her—though to be more exact she did the splits in front of my car and slithered ungracefully beneath my bonnet. She can't be badly hurt—just the ankle. Must be all of twelve stone,' he grumbled musingly, 'no wonder my back's gone into spasm.'

'Eleven stone—just!' came an indignant and argumentative voice. 'And would you kindly let me know if there's anything wrong with me, or if it's just nurse's paranoia.'

Helen was smoothing the frowning brow, noting the dampness of the skin and the signs of shock in Staff Owen's face. 'Were you running for the bus, Maggie love?'

'Uh huh. Now I'll never get my hands on a cut-price pair of Italian shoes!'

Bram straightened from his examination and patted her shoulder consolingly. 'Treat yourself to some nice gloves instead—far cheaper. I'll do you a nifty line in plaster for your left foot, one of my Markland specials, choice of blanc de blanc or Paris white.'

'Really, Bram!' protested Helen clutching at Maggie protectively. 'Sometimes you can be so cruel.'

Maggie was pressing her knuckles to her forehead in a wearily resigned gesture. 'Would you credit it? I have to break my ankle to get myself picked up by Bram Markland.' She managed a feeble grin as Bram aimed a friendly punch that stopped six inches short of her nose.

'And break my back into the bargain,' he teased. 'What do you think Sister Guppy's going to have to say about this?'

Maggie looked at Helen and Helen looked at Maggie. Two staff nurses exchanging looks of foreboding as the implications of Maggie's untimely injury began to dawn. Helen would have to assume the responsibilities of senior in the department—and for however long it was going to take Maggie to get back on her feet again. And Maggie must face up to the knowledge that it could mean two months on crutches . . . her foot was turning a delicate shade of blue and swelling grossly.

'How did it feel when you stood up just then?' queried Bram with what Helen considered a ghoulish interest.

Maggie looked sick. 'Sort of . . . crunching,' she admitted.

Bram fetched a wheelchair and glanced at his watch. 'Let's get you along to X-ray before our radiographer disappears for the night. I think you may have several small fractures there.' He raised an enquiring eyebrow at Helen. 'Shall I get a porter, or are you going to wheel her down while I see if I can get hold of George?'

'I'll see to it,' said Helen quickly. She wasn't handing Maggie over to anyone else—the poor girl was white as a sheet now.

When the plates were ready, Bram looked most concerned. They were still waiting for George Raven to come and give his opinion as orthopaedics registrar. 'You'll probably need a whiff of gas, old girl. Look at this.' He pointed out three separate fractures. 'The fibula—just above the ankle there. Hairline fracture of the tibia, and the malleolus of the tibia. Classic Pott's luck, I'm afraid.'

Maggie groaned. 'That means a knee-length plaster, doesn't it? Oh Helen, I'm most desperately sorry about this. What a fool I was to try and chase a bus this weather.'

Helen gripped her hand and told her not to be an idiot. It was no one's fault—and least of all Bram's, she now realised guiltily. Jumping to conclusions where he was concerned was getting to be a regrettable habit that must be curbed . . .

Inevitably Helen was late off duty, but she rang home first and told them about the accident and to expect her when they saw her. Maggie had been transferred to a single room off the ENT ward, the only space where she could get a bit of comfort and privacy to lick her wounds. Although technically Bram was on leave, he had shed the jacket of his dark suit—presumably the one he had worn for the interview—and gone with Maggie and George into theatre. Helen had been too busy to help, much as she yearned to do so. And Maggie was in too much of a post-anaesthetic haze to appreciate a visit later that evening.

It was some time after nine-thirty when Helen got to the bicycle shed and shone her torch on the padlock as she unchained her steed. But, just as her key was searching for the lock, a heavy hand fell on her shoulder. A muffled cry of fright broke from her lips.

'Shut up, silly,' scolded a deeply familiar voice. 'You won't need that thing tonight—you're coming with me.'

She found herself pulled upright in the darkness as the torch was removed from her nerveless fingers and its beam extinguished. 'C-coming with you? What do you mean? I'm going home, Dr Markland, I've had a heavy day.' But the tall black shape forcing her out of the shed and across the car park, was not easily to be thwarted in intention.

'I'll scream. Let go of my arms . . . let go of me!' She might have been frail as a butterfly, for all the effect her struggles to free herself from the iron bands of his hands and arms were having.

'Go on then, scream. Be a little church mouse and shriek your whiskers off.'

Feeling awfully silly, but more infuriated now than frightened, Helen drew in her breath and filled her lungs . . .

'So you would too!' A little flurry of cloaked figures crossing between buildings were glancing their way with curious interest. Bram bent his head and next moment his mouth had closed over hers, kissing her till Helen's inflated lungs were fit to burst.

'That was totally unnecessary, Dr Markland. I wish I knew what all this is supposed to be about!' She wiped the back of her mouth on her gloved hand, but stood stock still, resigned to the knowledge that she was not intended to escape his clutches.

'I want to talk to you. Now seems as good a time as any. Get into my car and we'll go to my home.'

Glowering at his side as they drove the short distance along icy roads made unfamiliar by the coverlet of snow, Helen bemoaned the failure of her plan to avoid this assignation with Bram. If she had seen the cloaked figure watching their rear lights fade into the distance, she would probably have leapt from the car there and then. But not knowing they were observed, the best thing seemed to be to let Bram get the whole matter over and done with, whatever it was he wanted to say . . .

Numb with exhaustion Helen pulled her jacket collar about her ears and slumped back into the car seat, watching Bram's hands on the steering wheel as they guided the car to the place he called home.

It was about a couple of miles from St Leonard's, and in the opposite direction to Holy Trinity Vicarage, when

Bram turned his battered and elderly Ford up the drive of a largish house shrouded in darkness and surrounded by a variety of snowcapped evergreens. Helen gave a start and woke up a little. This was not how she had imagined Bram's place. This looked like the sort of pad a wealthy man might choose—and certainly not a bachelor doctor. But Bram was already out of the car and crunching across the crisp white ground to open her door. Unprotestingly Helen got out and stared curiously up at the handsome Georgian portico and fanlight, the steps leading up to a shiny fir-green door with gleaming brass knocker and letter-box.

Bram went ahead, switching on lights that revealed a hall with black-and-white tiled floor and the sort of antiques that could never be mistaken for reproduction. It was all rather grand, with oil paintings in gilt and maple frames, and untidy touches that suggested Bram had been in earlier and just dumped the things he had brought back from London. A pile of books and letters spilled across the hall table, a couple of holdalls had been dumped on the diamond-tiled floor. A striped college-type scarf dangled from the elegant curve of the banisters.

'In here,' ordered Bram, slipping the jacket from Helen's shoulders and propelling her with a hand in the small of her back into his den. Leather and rich dark wood. Crimson velvet curtains and a mahogany desk piled with papers and correspondence. There was an electric fire in a grate that cried out for logs and roast chestnuts and long-handled toasting forks. Lamps with gold shades made glowing pools of warmth on the dark-green walls, and in the alcoves Helen's eye travelled over white shelves crammed with books. Bram had his back to her and was standing before an open drinks cupboard clinking glasses. There was a loud pop and the sound of pouring liquid. Then Helen found a tall narrow glass pressed into her hand, its contents clear and golden and lightly effervescing.

'Champagne. You once said you've never had it before—tell me what you think.'

'Champagne?' said Helen stupidly. 'I thought that was for celebrating.'

'We *are* celebrating. I've been offered a Junior Lectureship in Surgery.'

'Wh-whe-when?'

'At the start of the academic year. That means I leave in June and take a couple of months' holiday. I've got a—that is to say, I'm borrowing a friend's villa on the Algarve. How about coming with me?'

Helen smiled into her drink and jumped as the bubbles tickled her nose. She pulled a face at her first sip, tested the second more adventurously, found that the more you drank the more delicious it tasted. Forgetting she hadn't had anything to eat since mid-day she swayed slightly on her feet and the bubbles floated lightly inside her skull. Forgetting she hadn't intended to stay—let alone sit down—she sank into the generous depths of the nearest chair.

'That's better,' approved Bram settling himself opposite so he could observe her smallest reaction. 'How does champagne suit you then?'

Dreamy blue eyes swivelled smilingly up to his. 'It suits me very well, thank you. But Dr Markland—I thought you were—um, I mean to say champagne . . . this house . . . everything in it. Doesn't really go with . . .'

Bram leaned forward, interested in catching every slurred word. 'Go with what?' he prompted gently, reaching for the emptied glass and refilling it from the bottle on the carpet at his side.

'Oh, you know. Crummy socks and holey sweaters and crumpled clothes.'

Bram grinned and handed her back her glass. 'Take it steady,' he warned. 'This stuff's not lemonade, you know.'

'You just don't dress like a rich man, that's all.'

He shrugged. 'You could say I'm a very relaxed dresser. Clothes don't interest me, and I hate shopping for them.'

'What about your car then? You should be driving a Jag or a BMW or something. Dr Markland, are you rather rich?' Helen sat up and stared at Bram as if she'd never seen a real, live, wealthy, man before.

He shrugged, as if he'd never really considered the matter before. 'I don't believe in parading my background. The house and the furniture—well, that's an investment and a lot of this stuff was left me by my grandmother. A car is just a car. It gets me from here to the hospital, that's all I ask. But my career I really am rather proud of—I haven't got that lectureship because of Eton and Cambridge.' He rubbed his hands in relish: it was going to be most enjoyable and stimulating— teaching medical students, while at the same time being allowed increasing opportunity for specialisation. Just one more thing was needed to make life perfect: and that was in the room with him that very moment. He looked across at Helen possessively. More than any other woman on earth it had to be this one . . .

Helen's eyes were huge and blue and wide. Her hair looked as if at any moment the holding pins would give way and the golden mass of it all would tumble over her oatmeal shetland sweater. She still wore her black stockings but instead of the trousers she generally preferred for cycling home she was wearing a short slim skirt that clung to her hips and thighs in nutmeg-brown cord. She had slipped off her boots, awed by the grandeur of Bram's stately hall, and her feet were tucked up beneath her. Bram thought she looked relaxed now, and adorable . . . and ready.

'Have you missed me this week?'

Helen looked at him over the top of her glass. 'We all missed you. Honestly, I never realised what a difference it could make with you away.' Suddenly her face fell. 'Does Elsie Guppy know you've got the job? She's going to miss you, Bram.'

'No one knows—except you. I was just driving back from London and stopped to pick up any post in my pigeonhole. That was when Maggie decided to throw herself in my path . . . it wasn't my intention to see you tonight.'

Helen stared down into the depths of her glass. For some reason she felt it wasn't safe to meet that mahogany gaze head on. 'That letter you sent me . . . you shouldn't have. What could you and I possibly have to discuss? Paul might have seen it—and then I should have had some explaining to do.'

He still sat there, that riveting stare turning her bones to water, contemplative fingers exploring the line of his determined chin. 'I wondered if you would try to avoid me,' he said slowly. 'That's why I thought I should grab you tonight, bring you here . . . Do you want to ring home? Let them know you're going to be late?'

She gave a quick shake of her head, aware of the tension that had sprung up suddenly between them. Drained her glass for something to occupy her trembling hands. Held it out defiantly for a refill—perhaps she should be going now though—drew it back and got to her feet in one graceful swift movement . . .

Bram rose too, towered over her, his shadow rearing dark against the light. Next moment (Helen couldn't explain how or why or what she had done to capitulate) she was in his arms and almost fainting at the intensity of his passionate kisses and the way her whole being responded in a way she could never have believed possible.

'Stay with me, Helen,' Bram was murmuring seductively into the velvet-soft skin of her neck. 'Stay with me tonight. Stay with me . . . for ever!'

He lifted her in his arms, just as he had lifted Maggie earlier, but with very different intent. Laid her upon the smooth cushions of the leather chesterfield as gently as though she were the most precious Dresden china. Helen's eyelids flickered hypnotically, her senses over-whelmed with the wine, with fatigue, with the onslaught of his ardent mouth and skilful hands. Helpless in the tidal wave of her own responses, submerged and drowned, no more a sane and rational being . . .

. . . there never was a man like this man; with him pleasure and joy were indescribable, beyond words, beyond expressing, beyond even her wildest most un-censored dreams.

As Bram lowered his body over hers, the warmth of him, the unfamiliar masculinity, the long hard weight of him, engulfed and enfolded her, his mouth murmuring the most impossible promises and endearments. All that she longed to hear in the secret recesses of her heart and mind. A lost, enchanted sprite, ensnared in the fasci-nating tangle of shadows surrounding this giant who bestrode her world.

Then, just as she was on the point of drowning irrevocably, a glimmer of sanity began to draw Helen back towards the surface and the harsh reality of fact . . .

'You're mine at last!' Bram was exulting, in the discovery that after all this was not an unattainable love. The one girl he had believed he could never have was on the point of surrender, body and soul. The one girl he needed more than any other in the whole wide world. 'Darling Helen, all these years I've been searching for you. And then when I found you I thought . . . I never believed . . . Nothing shall come between us now. I would have lied, and murdered and stolen to get you!' This was not strictly true, but Bram was in such a state he was hardly aware what he was actually saying, and so carried away with triumph and excitement that he probably believed it to be true. 'Lied and murdered and stolen,' he repeated joyously, 'if you had not come to me of your own accord.'

This was a mistake.

Helen's head broke the surface of reality. Of her own accord? Never. Not while she had made that promise to Paul . . .

In the space of seconds she changed from a quivering, sensational being, to one shocked and weeping and stone-cold sober. Determined to fight Bram off, whatever the cost, with flashing eyes and tearing fingernails. Appalled by herself as much as by his attempted seduction, appalled by the whole unbelievable scenario.

'Hell's teeth!' Bram's voice was a husky growl of pain and outraged disbelief at Helen's shocking volte-face. His hands were raised against her in self-defence, fending off this violent snivelling harridan lashing out at him in cruel despair.

The fingers of his left hand explored the burning slash which rended his cheek in a livid scar. He looked at the smears of blood on his fingers and the astonishment became a dull disappointed chill.

'If that's how you want it!'

He was far far stronger than she was . . .

Helen found herself dragged from the couch and swept up against the unyielding wall, pinioned there helpless as a butterfly on a lepidopterist's needle. Her face set in disbelief, her pale hair tumbling across her eyes like a starlet in some Hollywood thriller. Though Bram's hands held her with relentless force his lips sought out her forehead for a fleeting regretful caress. His breath was steadying now, though Helen's slender frame was wracked with shuddering gasps.

'I want to go home. Please,' she said like some ever-polite child at a party no one was enjoying. She turned her head away so the tumbling hair concealed her face. 'Please let me go home.' The pain in his eyes was too hard for her to bear. Those droplets of blood on his sallow cheek, blood drawn by her own shocking, violent, desperation. All this, all this because of dear, gentle Paul.

As though he read her thoughts and derided them, Bram gave a mirthless bark of cynical laughter. 'We didn't choose each other, Helen. Life doesn't work out like that—and neither does love. You wish you didn't love me—but your heart knows the truth. And, God knows, I don't know why it has to be you for me when I'm going to have to fight to get you!'

He released her, walked away, sat down staring into nothing. He seemed as if he might be talking to himself. 'I could have anyone—so why you? You're trouble. You're a nuisance. You're not even specially glamorous. And you've got yourself tangled up with quite the wrong man already.' He turned his head slightly, watching

Helen through narrowed eyes; and she bit her lip, knowing full well he was treating her like just one more clinical problem—the kind he solved so effortlessly and with such skill as part of his everyday working life.

'Take me home,' was all she would repeat, her face sullen and her eyes veiled. She wouldn't even use his name, as if her tongue might betray her struggling feelings for this tormenting mesmeric man.

But Bram had the last word as he dropped her in a darkened street far enough away from the vicarage to be discreet. 'Don't imagine this is all over, Helen. Because I'm warning you, I never start something I can't finish. But I don't need to tell *you* that, do I?'

CHAPTER NINE

WHEN THE postman called next morning, Jenni was beside herself with excitement, racing up the stairs and bursting into her sister's bedroom waving a clutch of official-looking papers and shrieking with delight.

'Wakey wakey! I've got an interview at the Royal Hanoverian. Isn't that wonderful?' She bounced on the duvet until Helen was obliged to tunnel out and take an interest, her head stuffed with what felt like damp cotton wool and her body protesting at being roused from deepest slumber.

'You might have brought me a cup of tea, our Jen. My mouth tastes perfectly disgusting.'

'Where did you get to then last night? Mum says your supper's still in the oven, all dried out and horrible.' Jenni peered more closely as her sister threw back the tangled weight of her hair and yawned hugely. 'You look terrible. What have you been up to, Hel?'

'Let's see that letter,' insisted Helen hurriedly, playing for time till she had her explanations and excuses polished up and ready for display. 'They've even sent you a map showing how to find the School of Nurse Education. There it is—right next to the Medical School, no wonder the Royal Han is such a popular place to train! Looking at this brings back some memories, I can tell you. What else have you got there?'

Jenni leafed through her sheaf of papers. 'Declaration of Health. Not that I've anything to declare, unless they count a sneeze or two of hay fever when the blossom is

144

out. Lists of certificates I have to bring with me for interview . . . oh look! including passport. Heavens to betsy! Where can I get one of those inside of a fortnight?'

'Passport?' echoed Helen, looking as puzzled as her sister was aghast. 'Here, give me that.' She skimmed the page until she discovered the offending passage. 'Valid passport—'if applicable', dumbo, can't you read properly yet?' She batted her sheepishly grinning sister over the head. If that wasn't just typical Dilly Daydream. The Royal Hanoverian wouldn't know what had hit them when Jenni walked in. But no applicant was more determined to prove her worth. And Jenni was one big tonic, she surely was.

'See my letter from the Director of Nurse Education herself?' If it had come from the Queen, Jenni could not have acted more proud.

Helen nodded and laughed, recalling her own joy when she too had got as far as being called for interview. Rejection was too awful to contemplate at this stage. 'There's even a full day's schedule printed here. Trust the Royal Han to be superbly well organised. Tour of the hospital, with slides to follow and information about the training programme. Coffee with the clinical tutors. Lunch—then medicals and interviews in the afternoon. Phew, what a busy day.'

Jenni snatched back her letters and pranced over to the door. 'I'm going to write this minute and tell them I shall be pleased to attend for interview. Or do you think I should say "pleased and proud"?'

'Pleased, I think, will do nicely, love. And be sure to use a first-class stamp.'

On his way down to the hospital chapel Paul was hailed by the porter, Jimmy O'Brien. 'Letter for you, padre.

Someone left it in the pigeon holes, but I said to meself, the padre will never look there so I'll bring it up to the desk.'

'Thanks very much, Jimmy. Very thoughtful of you. How's that slipped disc by the way?'

Jimmy leaned confidentially over the desk and beckoned to Paul to come closer. 'To tell the honest truth, padre, I've been goin' to see one o' them chiropracter fellows. And I'll be after feelin' a new man, I will. Now, he jumps on me back and me bones go crack, but afterwards—oh, the blessed relief.'

'Glad to hear it, Jimmy. You're a well man, that you are, I can see it in your eyes.'

Paul went on his way, chiding himself (not for the first time) for slipping into the speech patterns of whoever he was talking to. He grinned to himself as he opened the door of the small vestry using his bunch of keys, lifted the small brown attaché case he carried with him onto a small table, and without any special interest ran a hasty thumb beneath the gummed seal of the seemingly innocuous letter the porter had delivered personally into his hands . . .

Maggie was sitting up in bed, in a rosebud-print nightie with a big frill that was less than flattering to the broad plump shoulders it was meant to conceal. There was an open box of chocolates on her locker and a pile of glossy magazines on the hospital-green coverlet. She looked about twenty times better than when Helen had seen her last, peering round the door now with a breathless eye.

'Sister says I can have five minutes. I ran all down the top corridor without anyone seeing me! How are you, you poor old love?'

Maggie assumed a suitably martyred expression and

indicated the plastered mass beneath the bedclothes. 'Don't sit on that, will you, old girl. I believe I'm as well as can be expected. Off the critical list now, anyway.'

The two dissolved into splutters of muted laughter, with 'old girls' and 'old things' peppering the conversation so that an eavesdropper might have suspected they were listening to a couple of maiden aunts. Helen felt happier than she had been all day.

'Did you know, I've been doing some research,' stated Maggie importantly, 'and it's impossible to wee into a bedpan.'

'So *that*'s why you're being transferred to geriatrics. You've been wetting the bed, you naughty old staff nurse!'

Maggie stuck her nose in the air. 'How are you managing without me then? Not well, I hope.'

Helen looked serious. 'Say that again. We've got a male nurse down from men's surgical today, but he's only on temporary loan. When d'you think you'll be working again?'

'Have a choc to sustain you in the face of shocking news. I'm non-weight bearing for six weeks. So my brother's driving down to fetch me home, and I'll attend my local fracture clinic.'

Helen looked sick. 'Ye gods! I don't think I can bear it without you, Maggie. You keep my head above water.'

'Nonsense. You're as capable as I am any day—and don't forget you'll have Bram back at the end of the week. He came in to see me this morning, on his way to tell the powers that be he's moving on. He said he's working with you on Saturday, by the way, so you can kiss Gavin Wilson goodbye for me.' She rattled the chocolate box under Helen's thoughtful nose. 'Have another of Bram's chockies. I think he's getting to appreciate that an armful of big girl is better than an eyeful of Helen Westcott. More satisfying, anyway. Hey!' She leaned over to peer into her friend's pale face. 'Who's been knocking you about then?—you look terrible.'

'Oh,' Helen brushed aside the query. 'I just had a sleepless night—I do like your nightdress, it's terribly pretty,' she enthused, hoping to sidetrack the other staff nurse away from the drama she scented. Maggie chose to ignore that ploy, however.

'Isn't that strange,' she commented mysteriously, the twinkle in her eye so knowing that Helen was immediately set on her guard.

'Mysterious, Maggie? I don't see why?'

Maggie pursed her lips consideringly. 'We-ell,' she drawled with maddening slowness, taking her time in a way that had Helen writhing in torment . . . was Bram Markland going to turn out to be one of those men who got their kicks from kissing and telling? Without realising it Helen was biting her lips, a picture of apprehension, her fingers pleating the striped cotton skirt of her uniform.

'According to Bram, he's been having a fight with a neighbour's cat that didn't want to be stroked. There's this livid scratch all down his face, and any fool can see the shape of fingernails. Helen Westcott, if I didn't know you better I'd say you were actually blushing! Can you look me in the eye and swear you don't know anything about it?'

'Of course I can,' mumbled Helen as her throat constricted with the knowledge she had done such a dreadful thing to poor Bram. She hated violence of any kind; whatever *he* might have done, however badly he had behaved towards her, there was no excuse for carrying on like a barbarian. 'Anyway, I never blush—I don't have that sort of complexion.'

Maggie settled back comfortably into the pillows, knowing full well it was none of her business but too intrigued by this battling pair to let discretion get the better of her curiosity. Anyway, she had never subscribed to the hospital grapevine. Helen's secret—if she had one—was safe with her.

'If I didn't know you were engaged to Father Paul, I should have strong suspicions you might well be the girl most likely to put the "happily ever after" ending onto the legend of Dr Markland.'

Pretending a yawn and glancing at her watch, Helen patted Maggie's shoulder and straightened her coverlet. 'Well dear, sorry to disappoint you. But until they change the bigamy laws in this country, it's never going to happen.

'The very idea!' she added with a grin over her shoulder, putting her tongue out as a parting gesture of defiance as she left her friend's room.

You can go off people! thought an exasperated Staff Nurse Westcott as she pressed the lift button for the ground floor. Maggie had the most uncanny knack of putting two and two together—and coming up with an answer that sent an appalled frisson down one's spine! One scratched cheek plus one pale face equals a broken engagement and the final instalment in the long-running saga of Dr Markland's love-life. In real life, decent people did not jettison their promises and cause others heartbreak, just to satisfy their own shameful desires and longings for another passing love.

But, insisted the niggling voice of truth, that's just

what they do. It happens all the time. People fall in and out of love, and with the most impossible men and women. You can't organise love, you can't choose the direction of Cupid's arrow.

Unseeingly, Helen was following the maze of now-familiar hospital corridors, making her way with blind instinct back to Casualty. She felt like a casualty herself, a casualty of love, pierced and bleeding by Cupid's maliciously naughty dart. Loving two men in her shame—yet knowing there was really no choice to be made. Nothing was going to persuade her to reject Paul for Bram; it was impossible, could never happen. The dart must be torn out of her tormented flesh and rejected, now and for ever. There must be nothing more between staff nurse and doctor other than the professional satisfaction they enjoyed in their work together day by day.

Paul did a wheelie up the step and into the passage, careered dangerously down its narrow length, swung his racing bike round the corner to the right and braked dramatically outside the back door. On his own two feet again, he unfolded the length of his black cassock—which for cycling purposes he wore neatly folded up and tucked into the black leather belt at his waist, from which a small metal crucifix dangled from a short chain.

Though it was still freezing, he hadn't bothered with a coat of any kind since he had only come from the Church Hall a couple of streets away. He blew on his reddened hands and pulled off the cycle clips he used when he wasn't wearing tight jeans. And carrying with him that air of purposeful, vigorous energy which attracted people to him like moths to a flame, he strode through the vicarage and up the stairs to his rooms at the top of the house.

For a while there was silence.

Then the footsteps began, a thoughtful, meditative pacing, up and down, up and down; as though driven on by some deeply perplexing problem that incessant movement might encourage into a clearer light.

After a quarter of an hour—maybe longer—the door of his sitting room burst open and Paul came pounding down the stairs to Mrs Westcott's studio.

'Am I interrupting?' he queried, when the Vicar's wife called a rather bemused, 'Come in.' She was wearing tortoise-shell glasses with small old-fashioned owl-like frames, and they were slipping constantly down the bridge of her delicate nose. Her hair was ruffled as if her hands had run endlessly through it, and the hem of her flowery wool skirt was drooping down at one side.

'Fighting a losing battle again with that loom?' asked Paul sympathetically, setting aside his own problems as inappropriate in the face of Margot's more practical difficulties. He was quite used to getting roped in to hold this and hang onto that, and 'just turn this handle while I untangle the mess I've got myself into.' 'Now what can I do to help?'

'Paul dear, if you could just stand over here at the back of the loom and wind the wool on while I pull these threads straight. That's lovely dear, you've come just in the nick of time.' She showed him how to slide long slats of wood between the wool and the rollers and seeing how busy she was and absorbed in her work, Paul did as he was asked and didn't bother her with the problem he had intended to lay at her small wise feet. Perhaps, he decided with a sigh, it was for the best after all. Some things you have to work out in your own way and your own time . . .

'Paul?' Margot asked as he went across to the door with uncharacteristic leaden tread, 'was there something you wanted me for?'

He turned and smiled cheerfully, making a small dismissive gesture with his hand. 'Nothing important, just wondered if you were in, that's all.' He smiled, but the upper part of his face was in shadow from the lamplight across the room, and his eyes were sad.

'You sound tired, dear. Give me five more minutes and I'll make us some tea. I've been baking today and there's a coffee sandwich and a date and walnut loaf.'

Later, after tea with Jenni and her mother in the kitchen, Paul sat down at his makeshift desk and drafted a very important letter. A letter he never dreamed a few hours earlier that he would be writing that day. A letter that was going to change the whole course of his life . . .

Once written, he seemed to cheer up once more, to be his usual self when Helen came up that night to make the bedtime cocoa. She found him stretched out on his battered velveteen sofa, grinning over an article in the *Church Times* which claimed that clergy families lived in conditions of apostolic poverty, while his cheap record player reproduced a crackling version of Samuel Barber's Adagio for Strings.

'Don't you find that music rather melancholic?' asked Helen, depressed by the downward cadences of heart-rending violins. She had retreated into her emotional fortress, only to find stony walls set into foundations of shifting sand, ready to tumble at the first discernible weakness.

'Not at all,' countered Paul, handing her the paper to

read for herself. 'I've always considered the Adagio particularly soothing. By the way,' he moved to make room for Helen beside him, plumping the cushions for her and patting the seat with an inviting hand, 'I popped in on your Maggie Owen this afternoon after I'd been visiting on the wards.' He put a comfortable arm about Helen's shoulders but made no move to kiss her, and it was Helen, surprised, who snuggled up and planted a warm kiss on his stubbly cheek, taking his hand and enveloping it in hers. With Paul it was so easy to feel safe, cared for, relaxed. He was so easy-going and untemperamental. Just like Helen herself in so many ways.

'That was nice of you. I sneaked up for five minutes or so. Maggie seemed fairly cheerful, all things considering. Bram has pulled out all the stops for her, and she's getting VIP treatment.'

The shadow that flickered across Paul's face was gone in an instant, too brief to be commented upon. All the same, Helen noted it and was troubled.

Paul gave her a squeeze. 'There's the most tremendous match on Saturday. I shall need you to be there, urging me on from the sidelines. Oh boy—that should be one ace game!'

Helen pulled pack her head and looked up into his face, transformed now with that expression of boyish eagerness that was at one and the same time endearing— and infuriating! 'Darling, have you forgotten I work Saturdays now? Much as I'd love to, I simply can't be there. Sister's away this weekend, staying with her cousin in Middlesex, and with Maggie *hors de combat* there's no one I can do a deal with.'

Paul shrugged good-naturedly. 'Not to worry, sweetheart. I shall survive my disappointment.'

'You will take care, won't you, darling?' Helen slipped off the couch and knelt, clasping his knees and gazing at Paul with anxious eyes. 'I don't know what's worse. Standing there watching you all mauling each other viciously. Or biting my nails in the Unit wondering if the next ambulance siren's blaring for you!'

Her fiancé cupped her earnest face and kissed the tip of her nose with affectionate nonchalance. 'If it makes you happy I shall play like a lamb . . . probably get my head kicked in by all those wolves in rugger boots, but if that's what you really want—'

'Paul Hume, you are incorrigible. Now where did I put that pint of milk I brought upstairs?' Helen pulled away and scanned the room, sitting back on her heels. There, she'd left it just inside the door on that bamboo table where Paul left his post. Unfortunately in the half-light she had set down the bottle on top of a letter addressed to . . . Helen concealed with difficulty the leap of surprise in her breast as she saw the inscription on the envelope. The Right Reverend, the Lord Bishop of—heavens! Paul must be writing to ask the bishop to take part in their marriage service. He must then have a definite date in mind—and the hope of a parish of his own. Funny he should have said nothing, and neither had her father. They must be waiting to surprise her.

Helen looked across at Paul, but he was stretched out, his hands steepled on his chest, his eyelids closed. There was the faintest circle on the envelope where the bottle had stood, and she blew on it, hoping her warm breath would dry it out, rubbed gently with the soft pad of her fist. Yes, that should disappear all right, she decided in relief.

'What sort of a day have you had?' Paul asked lazily,

his eyes still closed. Helen was adding a spoonful of sugar to his cocoa, mixing it together with a drop or two of cold milk, careful as ever in everything she did. Her private thoughts welcomed the interruption; fascinated, dreadful threads that kept on struggling through crevices in the fortress wall and snaking their way back to Bram Markland; dwelling on his lips and his arms and his wicked, wicked words . . .

'Busy—as ever. Two people BID from a fatal car smash. They went straight down to the mortuary. Kiddie ran through a patio window—that was an awful case.'

'Will the child survive?'

'Oh yes, thanks to the prompt treatment of the ambulance staff. Bit of a bloody day, though, one way or another.' Helen sat cross-legged on the carpet, her cocoa on the floor beside her. 'We had one case that really was sickening. A middle-aged couple, more concerned with protecting the upholstery of their precious new car than preventing the wife's mother exsanguinating!'

'Good grief—had she cut her throat then?' Paul looked as if he'd quite lost the taste for cocoa, and Helen remembered she must tone things down for his queasy stomach. You got so accustomed to dealing with situations that would have the average man or woman in the street turning pale and giddy just contemplating.

'No love, that was a bit of an exaggeration. All the same, it just needed a bit of basic commonsense and first-aid knowledge to save the poor woman a deal of shock and discomfort. She had burst a varicose vein and they stuck her leg in a bucket and sat her in the car to bleed freely as you please—as long as it wasn't on their precious new upholstery.'

'And what they should have done,' interrupted Paul, 'if I remember from my St John's Ambulance classes, was apply direct pressure over the bleeding point and elevate the leg to slow the flow of blood.'

'Exactly. Sister didn't half tear them off a strip, letting her bleed like that into a bucket like a stuck pig. Good job Bram wasn't around—he's never one to suffer fools gladly.'

'Ugh!' Squeamish though he might be, Paul had in his youth gone to first-aid classes, as a responsible future citizen intending to spend his life working with and among people. In the space of twenty minutes, he found himself noting, that's the second time that man's name has cropped up. Clearly the tempestuous surgeon was much on Helen's mind.

'Isn't it good news about Jenni being called for interview at the Royal Hanoverian? The dear thing couldn't be more thrilled if she'd come up for the big one on Ernie.'

Helen frowned. 'All this excitement is a bit jumping the gun, don't you think? Even if they like her and all goes well, she still has to get that Biology O-Level.' A skin was forming on her cocoa and she spooned it away with a little moue of distaste.

'Do you think she could fail again? After all that extra coaching you've been giving her?'

She shrugged. 'Who can say? Everything depends on whether she likes the exam paper and gets some straightforward questions.'

Back in her own room Helen brushed out her long hair ready for bed, tossing it back from her face and staring at herself in the mirror. Although she was standing there in just her lacy white bra and pants, she didn't even notice the cold, absorbed in looking at her own image through the eyes of someone else. Bram's eyes.

There was so much Paul didn't seem to see; things that Bram's eagle eyes never missed, searching through into her heart and soul, and making no secret of his fascination. If only Paul could be more romantic, more interested in making her aware of herself as an attractive and desirable woman. Which Bram Markland did—all too successfully.

Helen stared at herself, puzzled and critical. Nice thick blonde hair, natural, not out of a bottle; not even highlighted by a clever hairdresser, just streaked by last summer's sun. Long pale stem of a neck, and shoulders with the delicate bones showing now she'd lost that bit of weight again. A nice figure, but hardly eye-catching with its long legs, tiny waist and swelling bosom. There were hundreds of girls, the same shape, the same weight, just as fair and blue-eyed—and probably with bags more personality and pizazz. So why did Bram want her above all the rest? After all, he himself had admitted she wasn't exactly a glamour girl . . .

She climbed under the duvet and switched off the bedside lamp, staring up into the soft smudgy darkness. There was only one possible explanation. It had to be because she was the one girl not available, a challenge to his egotistical self-satisfied nature. Oh, granted he had a lot to be self-satisfied about. He was clever, confident in his professional life, never rejected in his love-life. Love life! Helen almost snorted aloud in disparagement of the term. Bram Markland didn't know the first thing about love. He might have a little black book that ran into volumes, and he might be an expert in seduction techniques. But he didn't know the most important thing of all—and that was how to make a woman love him, or how to love in return.

And satisfied for the moment in her self-deceit, Helen closed her eyes and retreated behind the portcullis of her fortress.

CHAPTER TEN

ON SATURDAY morning John Owen loaded his temporarily crippled sister into his Volkswagen and headed north and homeward.

Helen was busy down in Casualty, her calm and tranquil nature quite restored.

Until Bram Markland hove into view with an ugly slash spearing down the left side of his face.

With a look of plain horror at the evidence of her own tempestuous handiwork, Helen made a strangled excuse and rushed into the safety of the sluice, burying her head in remorseful hands and forcing herself to take deep, slow breaths . . .

Bram made no attempt to follow—for which she was duly thankful. But all the same, at the earliest opportunity she must apologise. Even if it was Bram Markland's own fault.

Everything was Bram's fault. Long sleepless hours, during which Helen tried to analyse why she was not more over-joyed at Paul's letter to the bishop. No tattoo of triumph being drummed out by her treacherous heart. Now it was Bram who speeded her pulse and made her hands and knees tremble at the sight of him—as they had never done for Paul. Paul was safe. Paul was her best friend. Paul was the man she was going to marry.

A real and pitiless pain squeezed at Helen's heart. It weighed her down, mis-shapen and heavy as though filled with stones of calculus. Considering this, Helen's mouth twisted in a self-mocking grin. 'Pull yourself together, Staff Nurse Westcott, and just concentrate on your work. The universal panacea for psychosomatic symptoms! Nursing means total involvement for you—you'll soon forget your heartache in the bustle of the day!'

So, concentrating on presenting her usual cool un-flappable image, Helen did as instructed by Sister Guppy, spending the first half of the morning organising the junior nurses, and assisting Bram for the later part. He had greeted her with a knowing wink, grinning wolfishly as she turned troubled blue eyes away from the sight of that angry scar, veiling her thoughts with those fascinating sooty lashes.

It took all of Helen's self-control to keep her hands steady and hang on to her straining nerves.

She was just going off to lunch when one of the student nurses popped her head out of a cubicle and called her back. This was a girl who lacked confidence and needed encouragement to use her own initiative.

'Staff. Can you take a quick look at this lad for me? Dr Markland's gone to lunch and Dr Robards is busy in the plaster room.'

Helen indicated to the nurse to move out of earshot of the patient waiting hidden behind the screen of curtains. 'What is the problem, Nurse?' Helen was herself barely eighteen months older than this girl, but her manner was far more assured and professional.

'This lad, Pete Hammond, says he's a pop musician. Plays electric guitar with a group. You should see the colour of his hair, Staff, you'll get a real shock.' Haydee giggled and Helen concealed her impatience with dif-ficulty. 'During practice sessions he's been stuffing his ears with chewed up bits of paper. To cut down on the sound!' the nurse added gratuitously.

'Well, I didn't suppose it was some new method of feeding, Haydee. So why can't you deal with this yourself?'

Haydee scratched her head and looked slightly ashamed. 'Sorry, Staff. But everyone's been having a go at the kid's ears—with matchsticks and cotton buds and what have you. The paper's wedged in tight. His mum spent a couple of hours with tweezers and she sent him up here because their local health centre can't give him an appointment before Monday. And I'm afraid Pete's a very reluctant customer. He won't hold still for a moment.'

He wouldn't hold still for a staff nurse, either, but twisted his crimson and yellow head, groaning and complaining as if the two girls were threatening him with grievous bodily harm.

Helen's feet were aching and her insides yearned for a plate of good hot hospital stew. She wondered how the skinhead had managed to dye his head to look like a flaming tennis ball, the front a curving sphere of red, the back section brilliant saffron yellow. In its way, it was a work of art. Under her hands the shaven head felt sort of prickly, like soft stubble with razored scars running through.

At length Helen stepped back in exasperation. 'Look here, Pete. Why did you bother to come up to Casualty if you won't let us near your ears?' You great bald baby, she added crossly to herself. I'll give you one more chance.

She put her knee up on the couch cover and indicated to Haydee to get the other side and grasp hold of the youth's head. But before she could get a purchase on the impacted debris, Pete had let out the most blood-curdling shriek and clapped both hands over his ears.

'This is ridiculous,' scolded Helen. 'What am I to do with you, you silly boy? How old are you supposed to be—eighteen, or three? Well, if you won't co-operate I shall just have to—'

At that moment there was a swish of air as the cubicle curtains were swept aside, and Bram strode in followed closely by Andrew. They must have heard the fracas and acted on the instant, for before Pete knew what was happening he was pinioned onto the treatment couch and—half a minute later—a scar-faced doctor, who looked as though he was not accustomed to taking no for an answer, was dropping the superfluous contents of one reddened ear into a kidney dish, and starting on the other.

Pete hadn't even the wisdom to pretend to be grateful. 'You lot assaulted me!' he complained, as Helen heaved herself up from leaning across a pair of smelly jeans. 'I'm gonna tell the top guy around here,' he added in a defiant attempt to restore his wounded pride.

Bram's lips curled in derision. 'Get out of here.' A spark of red flickered in the centre of his narrowed eyes. 'Out! Before I kick your backside for you. And don't come wasting our time again with your silly tricks.' To add weight to his words, Bram took hold of the scruff of his denim jacket and propelled the teenager well clear of the treatment area, brushing his hands on his coat as he stormed back into view.

Helen bit her lip, feeling almost sorry for the hapless 'musician'. Being on the receiving end of Bram's temper was a fearful thing. Just watching that brief explosion gave her the shivers. All morning she had sensed the surgeon was ready to blow if someone put a foot or a finger wrong.

'Th-thanks, Dr Markland, thanks, Andrew.' She

smoothed her uniform and checked her cap with un-steady hands. 'I thought you had gone to lunch,' she murmured, still avoiding a head-on collision with Bram's accusing eyes.

Cold fingers gripped the bare flesh of her arm, just above the elbow. 'I thought we might eat together.'

Oh dear, realised Helen, I've suddenly lost my appetite. Now where on earth could that have gone to? 'I—er, I wasn't going to bother to go to the canteen. I've an apple and some crispbread in my locker.'

Inclining his head so that his breath fanned her tense cheek, Bram's intimately possessive tone sent pins and needles rushing down her spine. 'You're getting too thin, my dear Helen. I prefer my women to be . . . all woman. When you wore that red dress you were quite perfect.'

They were out in the corridor now and Helen was painfully conscious of the curious glances they were attracting. 'Please leave go of my arm, Dr Markland. People are staring!' Really, even for him, Bram was in the most extraordinary mood; witness the brutal tongue-lashing which sent a sulking teenager off with his tail between his legs. Bram—who was usually quick to flare—and as quick to subside, radiated an electric tension that almost crackled. He had no intention of allowing Helen to escape: he would corner her alone at a quiet table, and she would be forced to listen to words she could not bear to hear.

There was one sure but dangerous way to stop him in his tracks. Helen wrenched her arm away in a last desperate show of strength against the remorseless doctor. When she stood stockstill, he too was obliged to halt. 'We've fixed the day. Paul and I. We're getting married . . . this summer!'

Instead of deflating, however, Bram seemed to swell and grow monstrously tall as he towered over her, heedlessly blocking the busy corridor. People stepped round them—their eyes flicking from Bram to the ashen-faced staff nurse who was nervously twisting her hands and bowing her neat blonde head. It probably looked as if Helen was getting a good and proper dressing-down for seriously displeasing one of the senior medical staff, glowering down at her with his arms akimbo and his bottom lip out-thrust in temper.

Then, swinging about on his heel Bram loped away on those long lanky legs, his shoulders hunched and brooding, like some powerful bird of prey in search of other more willing victims.

He was not to be seen in the dining room. Had he been there Helen might have screwed up the courage to sit with him and try to talk things through; to persuade him his anger was unfair. Bram was piqued, simply because never, in all his exploits with the opposite sex, had he come up against a girl who was determinedly not available. One day he would meet someone, fall truly in love—and that would put an end to his legendary prowess. And thankfully he would never know how close he had come to breaking down all Helen's defences. The ache in her heart . . . well, time was renowned for its healing powers.

Helen had been working in the plaster room with Nurse Hedge when she heard Sister's raised voice in the corridor. 'Getting mud all over reception, are they? We'll soon see about that!'

They . . . mud . . . rugby . . . oh no! shrieked Helen's brain as the word-association conjured up a vision that speedily became reality.

'Can you come please, Staff?' urged a breathless voice

at the door of the plaster room as, wide-eyed with anticipation the third-year nurse who had been struggling earlier with Pete, conveyed Sister Guppy's summons. 'It's Father Paul, and Sister says you had better come.'

'Of course,' agreed Helen after one long calming breath. 'I must just wash my hands and get this apron off.'

The scene that met her astonished eyes was like something out of a farce. There was Paul, his arms across the shoulders of two brawny members of his team, hopping on one brawny leg. The three of them grinning and so thickly plastered with wet mud that every move left a trail of devastation over the gleaming tiled floors of Sister's precious department. Three huge filthy brutes, legs like tree trunks, white teeth gleaming ferociously out of faces caked in rich brown mud, one of them patting Sister with a gentle consoling paw and leaving his mark on her immaculate navy dress.

'Sorry about this, dear Sister Guppy, but I seem to have got myself damaged again.'

'*Really*, Father Paul? And was it altogether necessary to bring your team and half the pitch with you? This place has never been in such an appalling mess. My cleaning ladies will have a fit when they see what you three have done in the space of minutes!' Sister scolded and sighed and frowned, and told one of the nurses to bring a wheelchair quickly and take the injured chaplain into the two-bed treatment room, making sure he didn't touch or brush up against any walls or curtains en route. She shooed away his liveried retainers, who sauntered off laughing and cat-calling after Paul who thumbed his nose in return as he found himself being transported through the department in some style—with Sister

Guppy and an equally irate fiancée exchanging looks
that said more than words could convey.

'He promised me!' wailed Helen. 'You promised me!'
she tackled furiously, as soon as the rest of the staff were
out of earshot. 'You stupid great lout.'

'Ouch darling, that's a bit strong! Don't you agree, Dr
Markland?'

Bram had come in so silently that Helen hadn't even
realised he was there with her and Sister Guppy. Sensing
the amusement in the doctor's all-seeing eye, Helen
tensed defensively.

'If I may reserve judgment until I see what the problem is,' suggested Bram gravely. 'Wouldn't wish to
interfere with a lovers' tiff.'

'I'll just pop in and out,' said Elsie Guppy, nipping
off to keep an eye on things. 'You stay with Paul,
Helen.'

'Yes, Sister.' For some unearthly reason Helen was all
fingers and thumbs as she struggled with Paul's intri-
cately laced boots beneath the gaze of these two very
special men. Flakes of dry mud scattered over the
polished tiles and smeared Helen's hands and apron; but
for once she was unaware of the mess.

'You know,' said Paul agreeably with an air of mild
consternation, 'if I'd been involved in a ruck or a maul, I
could understand it.' He rumpled his already tangled
mass of golden curls with a perplexed hand. 'But there I
was—nowhere near the ball in play—just running up the
field and minding my own business. Keeping out
of trouble like I promised Helen . . . when crack!'
He shrugged, 'I'd suddenly lost the use of my left
foot.'

'Did you miss much of the game then?' commiserated
Bram, squatting down to make his examination.

Helen's exasperated snort fell upon deaf ears.

'Not really. Only ten minutes to go. Actually I was just congratulating myself on being in one piece, would you believe. Brilliant game though, Helen darling.' Paul's face was alight at the memory as he reached across to squeeze his fiancée's hand. 'You'd have loved it!'

'Can you cut his sock off please?' said Bram into the unresponsive silence. Helen sniffed and attempted to preserve the sock and her uniform. She had a good idea what the problem was from her own experience of casualty work—and Paul was in for a shock. But it was not for her to pre-empt the doctor's diagnosis. In the pit of her stomach lay a miserable coil of sickness.

The department was well used to coping with a steady trail of sports injuries, resulting particularly from contact sports such as Rugby Union. Treating them was a costly business in health care demands, for though most were simply fractures and soft tissue injuries, relatively minor problems in fact, it was just the same a considerable expense to provide the services necessary to diagnose and treat each patient.

'Fashionable at the moment,' murmured Bram, poring over Paul's damaged limb, 'these foot and ankle injures. First poor old Maggie—now you. Hm . . . let's see what happens when I . . . squeeze your calf, so. Any pain?' He glanced sharply up into the curate's unconcerned face.

'Nope!' Paul's admission was cheery enough, for there was no pain and so he assumed the damage, if any, must be minimal. 'As I told you, there was just this snap—like the cracking of a whip—and I went down on my face in the mud. Thought for a moment some guy had shot me!'

He had never looked more handsome to Helen than at

that moment, his golden curls all damp and muddy, glowing with confident vitality.

'Look Paul, I'm sorry to have to tell you this, but you've snapped your Achilles tendon.'

Helen winced, and Bram looked sympathetic as the young chaplain gasped in shock—then cursed volubly in a most unclerical fashion.

'Sorry old chap,' repeated Bram with a perfunctory but well-meaning squeeze of the younger man's shoulder, 'but there it is. We shall have to admit you, though God knows where I'm going to put you since we're crowded as Hades.'

Paul had gone quite white, and instinctively Helen reached across and grasped his hand. This was no moment for recriminations. The prospect of loss of mobility had clearly struck home with a vengeance. Paul was rubbing his forehead, with a helpless, disbelieving gesture. 'Can't a ruptured Achilles get better of its own accord? I mean, I'm pretty fit and reasonably young.'

Dr Markland shook his head. 'Unfortunately, it's mainly in older people that some heal spontaneously. In younger men or women the tendon may need stitching up. See this, when I squeeze your calf I am attempting to shorten the tendon. But because it has snapped—and remember you heard it go!—you cannot move your foot. I'm afraid I'm going to have to admit you for observation, and see what the specialists' verdict is on this one.'

Paul looked stubborn in a way that Helen had never witnessed before. 'And suppose I refuse?'

The two men's eyes met in a strange challenge that made her blood freeze. What was this? What was Paul doing? She grabbed at his hand again. 'Paul—don't be silly. Of course you must have the operation if that's the best thing for you. Trust Bram, darling. He's the expert. He knows what he's talking about!'

To give Bram his due, he looked nonplussed for a moment at his patient's unexpected rejection of treatment, then tried again.

'Look. Over the last six weeks we've had more than two hundred people requiring treatment for injuries sustained in contact sports. My advice to you is: accept our very experienced judgment, and once you've had the op. and you're on the mend, cut out the rugby, old chap. You could end up with a serious spinal injury before you've finished.'

Paul looked from Bram to Helen, and back to Bram again. He wasn't smiling when he said, 'Sounds as if you two are ganging up on me.'

'Rubbish!' exclaimed Helen much too quickly, her eyes filled with sudden alarm. 'You've always considered me a spoil sport—now you're hearing it from the horse's mouth.'

Bram whinnied and showed his teeth, coaxing a grin out of the disconsolate figure in the wheelchair, and ruining, in Helen's view, a splendid opportunity to convince her fiancé once and for all of the error of his ways.

'And I also hear I must congratulate you,' Bram went on unabashed. 'You're an exceedingly fortunate man, not that you need me to tell you that.' He delivered this with all the dignity of one who had at last resigned himself to the inevitable, and only Helen was aware of the flicker of that tell-tale muscle in his cheek which let her know the doctor was under considerable stress. She couldn't bear to look at either of them, but turned away to hide the sudden tears that welled and ebbed and threatened to overflow.

It was Paul's turn to look taken aback. He turned questioningly to Helen but she was preoccupied with the dressings trolley and had her back half-turned aside. 'Thank you, Bram. I must say I didn't realise you hadn't heard about Helen and me.'

Leave it there, Paul darling, leave it there, implored his fiancée with silent intensity. Oh, please don't say anymore because if you do, Bram's going to realise I made it up—and I shall look the most awful idiot.

But the fates, it seemed, were against Helen. 'She's very young of course,' explained Paul, wondering why she was excluding herself from this very curious conversation. If Bram really didn't know they were engaged, then perhaps . . . on the other hand, it was *impossible* to believe he was as ignorant as he pretended. Why, of course, they had even joked about the engagement at the time he has asked Bram to look after Helen and Jenni at the Valentine Ball.

'She is very young,' he repeated thoughtfully as if to himself, 'only twenty-two.' He dwelled fondly on Helen's back view, eyeing her as though she were a dumb little thing who couldn't speak up for herself. Her neck was a fragile stalk, and fine pale wisps of hair had descended from the carefully pinned pleat, trailing childishly over her collar. 'We're in no hurry to name the day—not until we're certain of a roof over our heads. I hope for my own parish within the next year or so.'

'Ah, I see,' murmured Bram, seeing indeed all too clearly for Helen's comfort. 'Very sensible of you both. I hadn't realised Helen was quite so young—scarcely out of nappies, one might say.'

'Indeed one might not!' came the swift retort as Helen discovered her tongue at last. Now there would be some

awkward explaining to do. Paul was clearly perplexed—
and Bram had that gleam in his eye that warned Helen
he was up to something. He would be waiting for the
earliest opportunity to catch her off her guard. Well, he
could make what he liked of the fact that she had lied to
him; whatever construction he put on it, encouraging his
pursuit was clearly not her intention.

In the event, Paul agreed to surgery after seeing the
specialist brought in for a second opinion. But since St
Leonard's was under such pressure for beds, it was
decided Paul should go to London, to a nursing home for
clergy. He would have his operation in one of the nearby
teaching hospitals, then move back to the nursing home
to recuperate. That way he would not be taking up a
valuable bed unnecessarily. His parents were both dead,
but he had a married sister on the Isle of Wight, with
whom he spent his holidays, and he planned to go on
there for the rest period advised by the doctors.

It was her sister Jenni who made Helen pause and take
stock of the direction in which her life was heading. She
had visited her fiancé in the no-frills nursing home in
Fitzroy Square, relieved to report back to the family at
supper that Paul was safely over his operation and
cheerfully anticipating convalescing with Cecilia and her
family at their farm-house near Ventnor.

Later, Jenni had suddenly looked up from the timed
exam paper she was supposed to be attempting under
Helen's supervision, and said, 'I do want Paul to hurry
up and get better. It's too quiet here without him—
worse than when Hannah went away to nurse. Honestly
Helen, when you two get married I'll go stark staring
bonkers left here on my own.'

Helen was checking her watch. 'Oh—and what about

poor old Tim, your smitten conquest? Doesn't he count
for anything?' She was mighty grateful to Tim Harding
for having taken the heat off her younger sister's
devotion to Paul.

Jenni was doodling idly on her scrap paper. 'You
know what I mean,' she pouted, scribbling a fair imi-
tation of Paul's noble profile. 'He's one of the family.
We're so used to him being around it's like missing your
big brother.'

'You're right about that,' agreed Helen with a smile. 'I
shall write again tonight and tell him just what you said.
We're all missing poor old Paul, and we want him back
safe with us.'

Wrapping herself in her duvet and propped up against
the pillows, Helen found a quiet moment at bedtime to
put pen to paper. 'Darling, this is just to say it was lovely
to come and see for myself how well you're getting on.
There isn't any special news—I was just going to come
up and make your cocoa. Then I remembered! I'm glad
to know the nurses aren't as good as I am with the
cocoa-mix! Jenni says hurry up home; it's like Big
Brother (not the George Orwell variety I hasten to say!)
having deserted the nest. The writing paper's like a
block of ice and my fingers are freezing. I forgot to tell
you—there's bluebells out and daffs under that old apple
tree. And the flowering cherry's nearly over. Spring is
sprunging, and about time too . . . oh why is my bedroom so cold?'

Finishing her short missive, Helen snuggled yawning
into the duvet, allowing herself a rare wallow in intro-
spection.

. . . those last few months at the Royal Hanoverian
had seemed such torment. Being so far away from Paul,
longing to get back to be with him. Even turning up

the chance of a staff job at her own beloved hospital! *Then* it had seemed she could not bear to live without him . . .

So why wasn't it like that now? Jenni it was who had put her finger on it. Somewhere along the line, their relationship had mellowed, turned comfortable and un-exciting. Brother and sister, rather than two lovers absorbed alone in each other . . . No, that wasn't quite truthful. That was never quite how it had been—always so many others who wanted to share Paul's time, his companionship, his warmth.

So when? or what? or who, had changed her feelings?

Always when her musings reached this dangerous stage Helen would rouse herself from inactivity, say 'No more!' and take up her busy life. Brooding on the impossible was a self-indulgence she could not allow herself: too dangerous even to consider. It was shameful enough to find herself searching for Bram when he was not immediately in sight; raking the corners of the department with eyes that yearned, a heart that lifted at the sound of his voice; hands that trembled if she found him watching her unawares with that quizzical tilt of an eyebrow, unfathomable speculation in the mahogany depths of his gaze . . .

Maggie came back, earlier than anticipated, sporting a double Tubigrip and with her left leg a fraction thinner than her right, and her ankle still a little swollen.

'I hear darling Bram is playing the field again,' she remarked chattily as the two staff nurses sneaked a hasty coffee in the sluice. 'Back to his old games, now he's got used to the painful realisation that you're not about to fall into his arms like a ripe plum. You know, Helen, I really thought you stood some chance there.'

'You're too generous, Maggie dear. What was I supposed to do with one superfluous fiancé? Pack him off to a monastery?'

'Ah,' confided Maggie with a knowing glint in her eye, 'Paul wouldn't have a broken heart for more than five minutes. There'll always be ladies queuing up for the privilege of comforting that young man, and taking home his filthy rugger kit. No need to commit him to a life of celibacy and regrets—your Paul could marry any one of hundreds, and be perfectly happy.'

It was perfectly true! Helen felt shocked—then hurt—then rueful. Paul was such a straightforward person—he'd love anyone who was kind to a three-legged dog! And his own nature was so gentle and considerate and loving. Just the opposite of—

'As for Bram,' Maggie was saying, 'he's easy to fancy—but hard to manage when you've got him. And I don't know that he will ever marry, now. He'll bury himself in his work and become an eccentric consultant. The sort of woman he's searching for, whether he realises it or not, simply doesn't exist. Even *you* weren't perfect because you were too ready to answer back, and that rocked him on his heels I can tell you. Still, you made him sit up and take a more than passing interest. And all credit to you, you really showed him he wasn't playing a fair game, trying to entice you away from Paul. You definitely let him know you weren't available!'

'End of sermon?' enquired Helen with breathless astonishment. 'I don't know where you get all your information from, Maggie Owen, but you seem to know more about my affairs than I do!'

Maggie tapped the side of her nose and winked. 'The onlooker sees more of the game, remember? And I get the feeling I've given you a bit of food for thought.'

Helen shivered as though a chill ran down her spine; the less time she devoted to musings and ponderings the better. She hardly recognised herself in this paragon of outraged virtue as described with such relish by the other nurse. At the time it had felt such a struggle against her natural instincts and emotions. But in the end she had succeeded. Bram was not making an overt play for her attention these days.

'And he's back to his old ways, you say?' she suggested casually, while her heart thumped wretchedly and the coffee stuck like glue in her oesophagus.

'Three different nurses so far this week. Though Anne Fallon's going round crowing that Bram's been dating her over a month now. That admittedly must be one for the record.'

'Where on earth do you pick up all your gossip?'

'Over breakfast.' Maggie stretched her arms and yawned languidly. 'Boy, but it's great to be back. One does miss all the goodies on the grapevine. Of course, I daresay Bram thinks he might as well make hay while the sun shines. After all, he can break as many hearts as he pleases—before he heads on for pastures new.' She watched with interest for Helen's reaction. 'Only three weeks to go.'

'Three weeks!' The other girl couldn't have looked more stricken. 'Three weeks—but I thought it was the end of May?'

Maggie shrugged and took Helen's mug away before she dropped it. Rinsing them under the tap she left them to drain on the side. 'Come on, old chap,' she said comfortingly. 'They say Bram's giving a big party. We'll all be able to kiss him goodbye properly then.' And with an arm round Helen's shoulders she steered the younger girl out of the sluice and into the corridor.

'Well I for one won't be at Bram's party,' muttered Helen, her eyes fixed on nothing, her steps obedient. 'No—I for one shall not be there.'

CHAPTER ELEVEN

JENNI WAS back from her interview at the Royal Hanoverian. Her father had collected her from the station and she had been chattering non-stop ever since. 'I was jolly nervous,' she repeated for the third time at supper, 'when I went in for the actual interview my legs were shivering. And they grilled me like the Gestapo. You might have warned me, Helen.'

Her sister shrugged unsympathetically. 'They were probably testing you out. You look such a fragile little thing—as if you couldn't say boo to a goose. I daresay you showed your mettle!'

'When shall you hear the result?' enquired Mrs Westcott.

'Two weeks' time.' Nervously chewing on a coppery curl, Jenni added, 'I assured them I expected to get my Biology pass, and they want us to send a photocopy of the result immediately it comes out in late August. If I have failed, then its ttzziittch!' She made a sawing gesture across her skinny white throat, to the accompaniment of a tragic expression of mourning.

'So, it would be a provisional acceptance until then.' Her father peered thoughtfully over his bi-focals. 'Why not apply to some other hospitals who are less demanding in their requirements? After all, you have started at the top.'

'Or a good Art School dear?' suggested her mother, ever-hopeful. 'I know one of the principal lecturers at the—'

177

'Mother!' This was interrupted with a glower that would have turned aside a charging rhino. Margot Westcott, however, was made of sterner stuff.

'You are exceptionally talented, Jenni. I don't pretend to understand why all *three* of my daughters have this vocation to nurse. In your case it seems in defiance of the talent God has given you!'

Helen intervened, with a tact born of witnessing this same conversation time and time again, with her sister becoming more entrenched with every battle. 'Did they ask why you want to be a nurse? It's one of the standard questions.'

Jenni was shovelling down cauliflower cheese as if her legs were hollow. 'Oh, you know, I mumbled something or other, I forget now. Hey, but listen to this, you'd have died. There's the Director of Nursing sitting there like grim death, with this other dame—'

'The Senior Tutor,' prompted her sister with a frown.

'Yeah, the senior whatever. Well, right out of the blue Miss Sugden raps out at me, "And what would you do, Miss Westcott, if I was to be sick, here and now, on the carpet in front of you? What would you do if I had *diarrhoea*?"'

'Good gracious!' exclaimed her mother. 'How extraordinary. What did you say, Jenni darling?'

Jenni spluttered into giggles, then composed herself and replied as calmly as she had at interview, 'I said, "First of all, Miss Sugden, if you had vomited I should check your airway, and then I should clean you up at both ends. It would be most embarrassing for you, but I should do my best to reassure you and put you at your ease." I swear they almost smiled, the two of them.'

She beamed round the supper table as the family burst

into laughter. 'Well,' approved her father, patting her hand and looking proud of his youngest, 'if they turn you down after *that*, then they simply don't deserve you.'

After supper the next night, the Vicar called Helen into the study, looking grave. When she came out her eyes were puffy and her face blotched with crying.

'What's the matter with you?' asked Jenni astonished, as her father sploshed the medicinal brandy into a mug and topped it up with hot coffee. Helen drooped in the doorway, her loosened hair falling over her crumpled face.

'Take that up to bed with you, darling,' the vicar suggested, kissing his eldest daughter good night. 'I shall pop in later and see you're all right.'

Ten minutes later Jenni was sobbing too.

'What's the matter with you?' queried Maggie next day. 'You look like a lovelorn panda!' Helen had the sort of dark rings round her blue eyes that generally resulted from a night out on the tiles.

'Didn't sleep too well,' came the vague response. Then all of a sudden Helen had burst into tears and was standing there sobbing her heart out, tears dripping onto her apron, and her limp hands making no effort to wipe them away.

'Lord above!' exclaimed a horrified Maggie. 'Let's get you into the office and away from all these prying eyes.' With the most perfunctory of knocks, she had Sister's door open and was hustling a weeping Helen into the room where Dr Markland and Sister Guppy were pondering over a mass of papers spead across the whole of the office desk.

'Can I have a word?' Maggie raised her eyebrows at

Bram in a tactful attempt to encourage him to leave Helen and Elsie Guppy on their own. Funnily enough, the sister half-seemed as if she had been expecting this. She got Helen into a chair and was soaking a wad of tissue under the cold tap . . .

'What is it? What's happened to upset Helen?' Bram frowned with fierce concern at Maggie's helpless shrug of incomprehension.

'God knows. I just pushed her in there for some privacy. All the juniors were gawping and the patients' eyes were popping.'

'Has someone died?' Bram simply could scarcely believe he had witnessed the cool assured Helen displaying such loss of self-control.

'Your guess is as good as mine. I daresay we'll be told when Helen's good and ready. Do you still want me to try and get her to come to your farewell party?'

Inside the office, Sister was comforting an already more composed staff nurse. 'Your father rang me early this morning. We're stunned, dear. Stunned and disappointed. And so sorry for you both.'

Helen blew her nose hard, and tried to summon up a watery smile to demonstrate her determination to pull herself together. 'I'm all right now, Elsie. I think it was just delayed shock . . . sort of.' She patted the kindly arm resting comfortingly on her shoulders. Squared them, to demonstrate her resolution.

'These things generally work out for the best,' the older woman observed thoughtfully. 'You won't thank me for saying that to you just now. But it is so. In the meantime, since we've got Maggie back, would you like a few days' compassionate leave? You have some holiday owing to you by now.'

Even at such a moment, Helen found herself thinking

of Bram—and how little time there was left. 'No no! I'll be fine, honestly. Far better to keep busy.'

'Good girl,' approved Sister Guppy, letting Helen get to her feet. 'I knew you could be relied upon not to overdramatise the situation. One thing I would like to say to you. I believe Paul suspects he's the wrong man for you—rather than that you're the wrong girl for him. If that's any comfort for you to think on.'

Helen lifted anguished blue eyes to meet Elsie Guppy's shrewd nutbrown gaze. 'But Africa! It's as if he wants to run away from me. Put half the world between us. For two whole years!' Her tear-stained voice trailed off into memories. That letter to the Bishop . . . it hadn't been about their wedding after all. It had been asking to test his priesthood under the most demanding circumstances. Putting their marriage right out of the question. Unless they should both feel the same way when he came back . . .

The next few weeks passed dully. Helen was an automaton, doing and saying all the right things, outwardly her usual calm self, inwardly leaden and without feeling. It was the only way she knew how to cope with the reality of losing Paul and Bram, both within weeks of each other. If she let herself think too deeply about St Leonard's saying farewell to its senior casualty officer—and appointing another to take his place—then the lead in her heart would turn molten, and she would be consumed and burned-up by her own anguish. It was a prospect more dreadful even than losing Paul.

Everyone knew about her now. She would scream if just one more well-meaning person reminded her she was very young and her life stretched ahead, a beckoning future stuffed with compensating pleasures. Scream and scream and never stop . . .

One glimmer on the horizon—Jenni had her place reserved in the Royal Hanoverian's School of Nursing. And she was doing test papers for Helen and passing every one with flying colours. She too tried to cheer her sister up, now they were getting used to the empty attic flat at the top of the stairs.

'You know, I think Paul went away because he thought you were deep-down in love with Dr Markland. He said Bram used to tease him about you; say he'd pinch you off Paul.'

'When?' demanded Helen, her scalp prickling with indignation. 'When could Bram have said such things?'

'Oh, I dunno.' Jenni ran her fingers through her tousled hair and sucked on the end of her biro. Helen had a white towel wound round her freshly shampooed head, and Jenni thought the white by contrast made her sister's eyes looked darkly purple. 'When Paul used to hurt himself on Saturday afternoons and get taken up to Casualty. Before you worked Saturdays,' she added as an afterthought.

'How do you know all this?' Helen demanded, alarmed and confused and not a little perturbed by young Jenni's revelations.

'We-ell. If you promise never to tell Paul we used to talk about you and Bram in secret. You see, Paul found this letter you dropped. That was after he fixed up for Bram to take us to the Valentine Ball, to test you both out, sort of. I was to report back and tell him what I thought.'

'And what did you think?' said Helen in a choking voice. 'No! Don't tell me, I don't want to hear any more.' She raced up to her bedroom and plugged in the hair dryer, switching it on to its highest setting so the noise would compete with the fever in her brain. So she had indeed been the one to raise doubts in her fiancé's generous trusting heart. Knowing this, how was she going to live with her conscience? Especially when Paul had gone away so she could make up her own mind—and Bram had no further interest in her.

Life's little ironies! Shades of the Thomas Hardy books she had studied at school haunted her now. How she once had wallowed in suffering with the ill-fated lovers who lived among those pages. Served her jolly well right to have come to this herself.

'Now I've lost both of these wonderful men. Bram knows my engagement's off—but he's made no move to step in and take Paul's place. No—he's well-satisfied with carrying on the Markland legend. He doesn't want me any more. And I have too much pride to let him know my true feelings—even though Paul's untied his noose and set me free.'

When Bram asked Helen, very quietly and privately, if she wouldn't change her mind and come to his farewell party, it wasn't pride that got in Helen's way and made her refuse the invitation yet again. She simply could not bear to be there, to see him with Anne Fallon—or any of the others. To have to say goodbye in public.

Faced with that gentle but adamant mask which he had been searching, ever since Paul left, for clues of encouragement, Bram finally abandoned all hopes of pursuit. Not a trace of concern at his going; not a glimmer to show she might miss him after all.

'No thank you, Dr Markland. I'm not much fun at parties these days.'

He nodded, understanding. Helen was *not* over Paul. It would be cruel and caddish to pursue the quest further.

He gave one slight inconsequential shrug of his shoulders and turned to walk out of her life; glanced back—and caught Helen staring after him with an expression in her eyes that made him catch his breath on a surge of adrenalin.

But, as quickly, the shutters came down. And Bram convinced himself he had been the victim of his own desires . . .

Helen came downstairs with her coat on and peered round the study door. 'Dad? Could you run me somewhere—if it's not too much trouble?'

Her father stopped typing and rubbed his weary eyes. Helen it was indeed, glamorous and glittering and quivering with tension. 'You do realise it's almost midnight?'

'Hurry up then, or the old Morris will turn back into a pumpkin!' exclaimed his strangely wild-eyed daughter. She looked as if she'd been at the cooking sherry, with her over-bright eyes and glowing cheeks. Of course, it was really this stuff the girls all put on their faces nowadays. Come night-time all three of them turned into glamour pusses.

'Now you're not to wait up for me,' warned Helen as they drew up in front of Dr Markland's brilliantly-lit home. 'I intend to be very late indeed—and I am nearly twenty-two.'

'Go ahead and enjoy yourself,' said her father drily. 'It's your mother who'll be anxious, not me. You've always had a sensible head on your shoulders. If I don't see you till next week I shan't worry.' Not much! he figured as his daughter trotted up the drive on those ridiculous high heels. But it was such a relief to see Helen coming out of her shell of pretending not to care.

Bram had to struggle through the noisy throng to get to his own front door. He almost lost a button off his ivory silk shirt, and his red bow tie was all askew.

'Hello Bram!' said Helen, suddenly shy at the sight of him, unfamiliar in immaculate slacks and matching shirt. 'You do look nice. Please may I join your harem?'

There was a time and a place for pride. And it wasn't here, or now. Her fingers itched to straighten that bow tie . . .

Bram gave a low whistle of surprise, shut the door behind him, and slung his cigar into the damp grasses where it extinguished itself with an indignant splutter. Next moment Helen was in his arms, both of them breathing too hard to dare to kiss in case they needed resuscitating with oxygen. 'Helen darling!' exclaimed Bram when he was a little calmer. 'I had almost given up hope. If you only knew how much I love you and want to marry you.'

'*Love* me. Want to marry *me*! You never mentioned anything about love before. I thought—' But her thoughts were stilled by the revival of all those disquieting emotions she had never experienced in the arms of Paul, and Helen just gave in to it all like someone starving for the foods of love.

Suddenly realising they were floodlit by the house for all to see, Bram drew her round to the back, and through the unlocked doors of a splendidly shadowy Victorian conservatory crammed with giant palms and other mysterious frondy things.

'Who looks after all this?' gasped Helen in wonderment.

'Oh—the gardener. I'll have to sell the place soon if we're to live in Hampstead.'

'Hampstead?'

'Yes,' came the nonchalant reply. 'I don't want my wife and children an hour's journey away from the hospital, do I?'

'N-no. I suppose not.' But Bram was kissing her again, greedily, as if he could never bring himself to stop. He seemed to have the future all worked out, and Helen's mind was one gigantic, fizzing cartwheel. In all her life, had she ever known such happiness?

'Please could I take my coat off?' she whispered timidly. 'I'm getting awfully hot in here.'

'Anything else you'd like to take off?' suggested her new fiancé hopefully.

'Later dear—when the party's all over.'

'Let's send them all home now,' suggested Bram feverishly. 'What a sensational dress. Is it couture?' He said this with such innocence that Helen was quite taken aback.

'You're not joking are you? Does that mean you actually *know* the sort of people who can afford designer clothes? Oh dear!'

Bram was turning her about, his hands on her shoulders. 'My mother made this,' admitted Helen defensively. 'One of my friends borrowed it and cut the back out. I had to leave it like that.'

From the front the high-necked black velvet sheath with its clinging long sleeves was seductively elegant. From the back it looked as if even knickers would be superfluous. Helen wore her golden hair loose and swirling in a gleaming waterfall over one shoulder. Bram resolved to rush out first thing on Monday morning and smother her in diamonds. Damn it all, he could afford it.

Helen was returning the scrutiny. 'May I just check your socks, sir?' she teased. Bram grinned and hitched up his elegant trouser-legs—to display crimson socks to match the still-crooked silken bow tie.

'Not bad,' breathed Helen. 'Not bad at all.'

'I hope to improve,' murmured Bram into the mass of silken hair as he drew her back within the circle of his arms, 'with someone to guide my dreadful taste in the right directions. It's been an awful strain finding the right person for the job.'

'Well, I'm applying,' she whispered. 'I hope you can interview me right away.'

But Bram's absence had been noted, and the search was on. Lights flooded the conservatory and first to discover the pair of them in a passionate and oblivious embrace was none other than Anne Fallon. She was the first to leave. And George Raven the last. Somewhere around four-thirty.

It was just as well the next day was a Sunday and that Helen was not expected on Casualty. The pair didn't emerge from Bram's bedroom until well after lunch, when Helen rang home to persuade her mother to invite them back for tea.

In the rush between Sunday School and Evensong, coping once more alone, the Vicar managed to squeeze in a very interesting half-hour in his study with Dr Markland. Apart from asking for Helen's hand in marriage in the most gratifyingly old-fashioned way, the doctor had some very useful suggestions for improving the church finances, offering to take out a most generous covenant to help them. He explained that he was an only child who had inherited substantial private means from his father, a merchant banker; that he could well afford to keep Helen in luxury without her ever needing to work again. That, not surprisingly, was not much to her liking. They had agreed that until children arrived she should pursue her own career, with a view to resuming nursing when family commitments should one day allow.

For a couple so newly engaged, mused LBW, they seemed to have covered much ground in their discussions; for he was unaware that Bram had given such matters deep thought, ever since he first met Helen Westcott and their personalities had clashed so dramatically.

'Why did you want to be a doctor if you had all that money?' questioned Jenni with the tactlessness of the ingenuous. 'After all, it's such a long hard slog to qualify.'

'I'm a workaholic,' said Bram with unapologetic pride. 'I've got where I have on sheer ability. Being a troubleshooter gives my ego a tremendous boost. People bring me their physical problems, and it's my responsibility to solve those problems through my own skills. You need a mighty ego to be a successful surgeon. It's a well-known fact. How else would one find the courage to take life-or-death decisions?' He gripped Helen's hand and his eyes never left her adorable face. 'When I first met Helen I knew here was the girl to tame me, to keep my feet on the ground—make my world complete. Puncture my ego when it got too unbearable.'

'Silly!' murmured Helen fondly, kissing the tip of his nose, and marvelling how this time yesterday the very idea of doing such a thing would have seemed incredibly impertinent. Yet here they were, gazing into each other's eyes like a couple of soppy kids. They'd even held hands under the tea table.

The parents had gone to church, leaving the three of them settled in front of the drawing room fire.

'I wish I could be certain we really aren't hurting Paul,' grieved Helen, staring into the flickering flames as if she could see a soul there in torment.

It was Jenni who had the last word as usual. 'Don't you fret over Paul. You two just had an almighty crush on each other, and it changed into something else, more like friendship than romance I should say. I must admit I had a crush on him too, and so did Hannah. Now we all think of him more like a brother. Anyway, Paul used to tell me lots you didn't know about. He said he really wasn't sure about settling down yet; that's why he didn't like it when you nagged him over naming the wedding day.'

Helen suppressed a sense of being hurt that Paul should have felt able to tell her little sister these things. 'Take your problems to Auntie Jenni!' she exclaimed mockingly. 'I don't know where my sister gets her insights into human nature, do you Bram darling?'

'Oh, I should say it runs in the family,' he observed quite seriously. Helen had never seemed lovelier, curled up at his feet, her hair tumbling over her shoulders in corny Hollywood style, not a shade of eyeliner or a blush of makeup on her fineboned face. Casual in her blue-check bush shirt and faded denims clinging to her lovely limbs like a second skin. Paul Hume, he mused, you must have been mad to step out of her life like that. Mad . . . or a saint.

'No,' repeated Jenni with a deep sigh of satisfaction as she watched those two love-birds making eyes at each other as if the rest of the world didn't exist. She poked at the fire, sending up a shower of sparks in the chimney, a secret pussy-cat smile on her heart-shaped freckly face. 'There's no need for anyone to worry about Paul. He's going to come back in two years' time . . . and he's going to marry *me*.'

But no one else was listening.

Mills & Boon

4 Doctor Nurse Romances
FREE

Coping with the daily tragedies and ordeals of a busy hospital, and sharing the satisfaction of a difficult job well done, people find themselves unexpectedly drawn together. Mills & Boon Doctor Nurse Romances capture perfectly the excitement, the intrigue and the emotions of modern medicine, that so often lead to overwhelming and blissful love. By becoming a regular reader of Mills & Boon Doctor Nurse Romances you can enjoy SIX superb new titles every two months plus a whole range of special benefits: your very own personal membership card, a free newsletter packed with recipes, competitions, bargain book offers, plus big cash savings.

**AND an Introductory FREE GIFT for YOU.
Turn over the page for details.**